the
wine
down

LOUISE
LENNOX

Cover Design © Bailey Cover Boutique
Formatting: Indie Pen PR
Editing: My Notes in the Margin
Proofreading: Yvette Deon
Beta Reader: Kate Elspeth
Series Managed by: Indie Pen PR

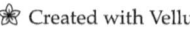 Created with Vellum

Blurb

Brandi...

Fearless

Southern

Broken

I'm the heroine saving farms from financial ruin and racism.

Who will save me from my loneliness?

I'm Too Busy.

I'm Too Hurt.

But it's homecoming weekend and I really want to WINE Down.

Except now, my family's farm is on the chopping block.

My best friend Riddick vows to fix it.

Because...

I'm the object of his affection.

And money is no object.

He wants me. But I don't want anyone.

I'm too fractured to put the pieces back together again.

But it's fun to feel Riddick try...

Riddick.

Dominating

South African

Billionaire

I'm the wealthy Restauranteur all the ladies love...

But I'm in love with my best friend.

Brandi doesn't want my love, but she does need my help.

She will get more than she asks for.

I'll destroy the past that's haunting her.

I'll own the present by pleasuring her.

I'll design our future; healing her.

She will be mine, and her heart will no longer hide…

Will Brandi Wine Down long enough to let love rule?

Can Riddick save Brandi's farm without killing their friendship?

Find out in this hot friends-to-lovers romance from Louise Lennox!

The Wine Down is a standalone, Friend to Lovers romance that is part of the multi-author series, Meet Cute Book Club series. Escape with this swoon-worthy collection of romances where meet-cutes don't only happen between the pages of romance novels and members find their own happily ever after.

Playlist

Love Poems by Bilal
Un-thinkable (I'm ready) by Alicia Keys
Mad Sexy Cool by Babyface
Lovers and Friends by Lil Jon & The Eastside Boyz, Ludacris and Usher
My Bestie by Lloyd
Make Out with Me by Maren Morris
Turn Your Lights Down Low by Bob Marley and Lauren Hill
Can't B Good by Janet Jackson
Don't Let Go (Love) by En Vogue
Feel My Love by Sauti Sol
I Like You by Lira
Can't Fight This Feeling by REO Speedwagon
He Proposed by Kelly Price
Be About It by Lira **(Brandi's Song)**

To my Great-Grandfathers Lucious Armstrong and Grant Frasier
Successful Black Farmers from a bygone era.
We will keep the land…And the land will keep us
Rest Well

Spring 2005

Brandi

I'M CHOOSING to change the world.

"You're choosing an elite finishing school." My infuriating boyfriend quips with a self-righteous glare. "Spelman College is just a large debutante ball waiting to happen. I'm disappointed in you Brandi."

I roll my eyes as I turn over.

"That's sexist Byron. You and I both know you're putting down the nation's number one Historically Black College and University because it exclusively serves Women. I thought you were smarter than that."

I slip from under his heavy arm to look for my bra and panties. I mutter a curse when I notice my favorite black lace thong by the door ripped.

Byron got carried away.

Our night started off hotter and heavier than usual. Byron's debate team took first place in the North Carolina state competition. The moment we got back to his apartment; he took me against the front door. My pussy cried a river when he whispered, *I'm going to fuck you until it's Friday.* Seeing that today is Thursday; those words promised a night of pleasure. In all, I got three shaking orgasms and a terrible fight.

We've had the same argument every night for the past year.

I'm leaving and he doesn't want me to.

I assumed he'd eventually warm up to the idea, but for the past year he's relentlessly campaigned for me to attend our local school, Abbott Ridge College, where he's already a sophomore.

Thankfully, my deadline to answer Spelman is in two days, and all his fighting will be for naught.

I'm going.

His frustration puzzles me. Byron Logan is Abbott Ridge, North Carolina's golden boy. He was captain of our high school basketball team, his class' valedictorian, and he served as president of the local young NAACP chapter. The latter is how we met two years ago. His passionate speech about helping Black farmers save their land from bad loans took my breath away. Everyone from here knows the Logan family. They have lived in Abbott Ridge for seven generations, so I always knew of Byron Logan. That night, I learned who he was. A kindred spirit.

The Logan home and farm, Dogwood Dale, used to be one of the largest cotton plantations in North Carolina. It was owned by the Talbot family. Byron's family was enslaved on that plantation until the Civil War. The Logan men were sought-after blacksmiths and the Talbots loaned them out to other farms. Byron's ancestors were allowed to keep some of that money, which they saved for generations to buy the entire family's freedom.

By the time Byron's great-great-great-great-grandfather saved enough to free his generation, the war was over. Every Talbot was dead from the war or a fever that ran through the town in 1864. The land went back to the county, and Byron's ancestors bought it for cheap. They've held on to it all these years.

Keeping the farm is nothing short of miraculous. Black farms are constant targets for racism. In 1920, there were over one million Black farms. There are less than 100,000 today. Byron reminds anyone who will listen that only 2%of the farms in America are owned by African-Americans. When I met him at that fateful NAACP meeting, I was waxing poetically about how we needed to make sure the five Black farms in our county filed to receive the reparations they were awarded in the class-action lawsuit *Pigford vs. Glickman.*

It meant a lot to me because I had watched my grandfather suffer for years. When he first took over the farm, the local bank gave him a USDA backed loan. Shadily, local banks wouldn't disburse the funds until it was almost too late in the season to grow crops. One year profits were so low we almost lost the farm. He filed a complaint with the USDA, but they did nothing, and the mistreatment continued. Year after year, my grandfather would watch as White farmers got their loans on time and Black farmers had their loan applications mysteriously delayed without explanation.

He watched some of his closest friends struggle and many lost their farms, homes, livelihoods, and reputations. When a Black farmer lost a farm, other farmers assumed they were irresponsible or just plain bad at farming. They would hesitate to even hire them as farmhands. The ones that stayed in town ended up addicted to drugs or caught up in crime. Somehow, my grandfather always seemed to make ends meet, but it all made him jaded and cynical. Whenever he was approached about filing more complaints, he would sneer that he had no time for politics.

When Black farmers across the nation got justice in that class action lawsuit my grandfather didn't blink. He told me all he wanted to do was work his land, but I encouraged him to file for his compensation. *"I told you Brandi, I got no time for politics."* I however, was tired of witnessing my grandmother's tears and his silent rage. I filled out the forms for him and began a campaign to make sure everyone in our region got their fair share.

I came to the NAACP meeting that night on fire for change. Instead, I left with a burning desire for Byron Logan. Apparently, I caught his eye too because he was so impressed with my words that he asked me to dinner. I was only fifteen and barely dating. But my family respected the Logans, so they reluctantly approved.

Two years later, I'm his girlfriend and it feels like he's trying to own me. He's studying pre-law at Abbott Ridge and wants me to follow in his footsteps so we can fight the power together. Sometimes, I feel he's the power I should be fighting.

But not tonight. I'm too tired.

"Buttercup!" he growls. "Stop playing and get your fine ass back in this bed. I promise you, what I have in mind will smooth your ruffled feathers. There's nothing to fight about; not really."

I look over my shoulder and try to hold my composure against his sparkling hazel eyes and mischievous grin. Byron Logan is fine, a flirt, and my first. *A deadly trilogy.* He wears his flawless butterscotch skin like an edible wetsuit. His basketball player body is long, lean and muscled. He looks older than his 20 years, but in the best possible way.

He's knocking Spelman because it's in Atlanta, a good five hours away from him and Abbott Ridge. He can't fathom that a school for Black women rivals any and every Ivy League in the country. It stands head and shoulders above Abbott Ridge. Spelman is where I need to be. The women there are world-changers and I already know what part of the world God wants me to change. Spelman can be my training ground.

Once I don my armor of bra, torn panties, and a T-shirt, I sit on the edge of the bed and face him. *I think better when I'm covered.* When I'm not, Byron's charm talks me into things like giving him my virginity under the moonlight at the beach.

That night it was too easy to let him slide my bikini bottoms off. The whole thing only lasted ten minutes, but it was life changing. I imagine it made me truly his, and that's something I desperately wanted to be a year ago. Now, I'm not so sure.

I hold my right arm out in front of me and shake my head. "No matter what you say, Byron, a decision as important as where I attend college shouldn't concern my high school boyfriend. The decision has lifelong consequences. Spelman is a higher ranked school than Abbott Ridge and it's in a city bursting with opportunity. I won't give that up because my boyfriend wants me to."

Byron lays back and folds his hands behind his head. In this position, his delicious pecks are on display. I hate myself for wanting to lick them.

I should be pissing mad.

He turns his head to look at me after what feels like forever. His eyes narrow to assess whether I'm worthy of his next words.

"I disagree. I think your boyfriend should be concerned about where you attend college…especially if he's in love with you."

I keep eye contact with him and my nose flares. "Bullshit!"

I'm not falling for any of his games right now. We always agreed we would never say those words to each other unless we really meant them. Byron knows I don't require them. Yet here he is, throwing them around like they're a magic wand.

He quickly sits up in the bed and reaches over to pull me close. Once my head lays against his powerful chest, the real emotional assault starts.

"I'm dead serious Brandi. I know I've never said it before, and that it looks bad because I'm saying it now. You have a decision to make in two days, and it may seem like I just want you here. I won't lie Buttercup; I do want you to stay." He kisses the top and side of my head tenderly, and I close my eyes to savor the feeling before he continues. "But I also love you and I can't imagine my life without you." He squeezes me tighter to him.

"Brandi, think of all the good we can do for the farmers if you stay in Abbott Ridge. We are an unbeatable team. It's fate. Can't you feel it?"

I bite my bottom lip and shake my head. I've thought that very thing at least once a day. I often feel Byron and I have a great work to do together.

"Brandi, if you leave, you'll be missing out on one of the best things in your life, and it will force me to do the same. I know you're my good thing. You're the one I can't live without, so please don't make me. Trust me with your heart as much as you do your body. I want you to be my wife."

The fuck! Is that a proposal?

"Wh-what are you saying, Byron?"

He doesn't skip a beat. "Exactly what I said. I want you to be my wife."

I suck in a harsh breath, and he looks down at me while stroking my hair back from my face.

"Brandi, this shouldn't come as a surprise to you. I always talk about our future together. I even told your grandfather that I plan for you to be my wife one day. You already know my parents love the match. The two largest privately owned Black farms in North Carolina uniting is an enormous deal. I'll admit that I wanted to wait to propose until I was at least out of undergrad. If you need reassurance, we can get a ring tomorrow. I'm committed to you for life, buttercup. Will you marry me?"

Shit. I hate this stupid tear for escaping my eye. *He wants to get married. Do I want to get married? I mean, no… I guess… maybe? He is a catch. Like literally THE CATCH. And our families will be so happy.*

I didn't know how much I wanted to hear Byron's beautiful words until right now. I promised myself I would marry my first and that my husband would be my only partner. It wasn't out of some bizarre sense of chastity or sacred virginity, but because it was one of the last pieces of advice, my mom gave before she died
.

I was thirteen and had just gotten my period. I'll never forget her words…Brandi, you're a woman now, make sure the only person you give yourself to is the one you can't live without.

She meant sex, right? She must have.

Byron knows this, and I wonder if he's desperately throwing those words back at me now to get his way. But when I look up into his eyes, he seems sincere.

Would it really be so bad if I went to Abbott Ridge College? I'd be near my family and Byron's right. I could do more for local Black farmers if I'm here. Suddenly, this feels right. All of it. Being in his arms, making love to him, and staying with him. *Marrying him.*

My future feels inextricably tied to the land we both grew up on and our families' legacy.

Abbott Ridge is my soul, and Byron is my heart.

That's my last thought as I hear the word "Yes." quietly escape my lips.

Friday: The Step Show

You cannot beat a drum with one finger
-South African Proverb

Chapter 1

Fall, The Present

Brandi

TATTOO PARLORS MAKE ME NERVOUS.

Abbott Ridge's downtown doesn't have much. Between the beautiful park square in the center of town where all our festivals take place, the eclectic Books and Beans Bookstore, and my best friend Riddick's Fall Line Restaurant; we do all right. However, the thing you notice most on Main Street is the colorful Ministry of Ink tattoo parlor. It's the coolest business on the block, by far. Despite my reservations about ink on skin, I'm proud of the funky little spot my sorority sister Daphne opened a few years ago. That's why I agreed to meeting her here today.

At the entrance I notice a vibrantly tattooed guitarist performing acoustic versions of West Coast hip-hop songs and I shake my head. "One never knows what they'll find at the Ministry of Ink," I muse, while my sister Ciara pushes open the door to the popular parlor.

She snorts. "You got that right. Your girl Daphne is special."

Daphne Abrams, the lead artist, and owner is indeed a special human being, in the best sense. I've never met someone as open and caring as my sorority sister. She services all kinds of people-*criminals included*- in her shop. A fact that makes the lawyer in me bristle when she's not waiting for me at the entrance.

Didn't I tell her I'd be here at noon?

"Brandi!" *There she is.* "Stop slinking by the door and come inside, for once. Let me lay some ink on your sexy skin. The work of my hands already blessed Ciara's."

Apparently, Daphne wants a proper visit.

I take a deep breath, walk in and smile as I embrace her. Ciara gives her a hug too, before making eye contact with a man the size of a mountain getting inked in the booth directly in front of us.

Good Lord, she's on the hunt.

Daphne also notices and throws Ciara a mischievous grin. "That's Seth Canton. He runs the Black Knights bar and motorcycle club. Want me to introduce you?"

Ciara makes a low humming sound in the back of her throat and fixes a stare on her prey. My sister is strikingly beautiful, often compared to Gabrielle Union in looks. She's also a brilliant writer. But her sexual appetite is insatiable, and she's a pro at locking her heart away.

Unlike me.

When our parents died in a car crash twenty-two years ago, Ciara and I were young teenagers that didn't know your entire life could come crashing down in a matter of moments. Our grandparents swooped in and gave us an amazing life, but they were never our spontaneous and cool mom or our loving but over-protective dad. We went from life in the suburbs to life on a farm. Not just any farm, our family's farm, Edenton Shores. A place that slowly became my lifeline.

Ciara dealt with the shock by deciding to not need or get used to having anyone besides me close to her again. That's why she easily flits from one relationship to the other. I craved the stability we lost and attached myself whole-heartedly to a creep in high school. I sought the steady, loving hand a daddy provides. At *least that's what my therapist says.* No matter the reason, I'll never make that mistake again.

I throw Ciara a look, but she only throws Daphne and me a naughty smile. I'm pretty sure the Black Knights are into some illegal shit. It doesn't matter though, because Ciara won't stick around long enough after she fucks him to be in any real danger.

"No, thanks Daphne. I got this. Why don't y'all go plan your little book club thingy while mama goes to work?" She adjusts her perfect breasts and saunters over to her prey. I shoot another look at the head of the Black Knights and catch a wolfish gleam in his eye.

Be careful, little sister, you may have met your match...

Shaking my head, I turn to Daphne and we break into a fit of laughter. Once we catch our breath, Daphne pulls me into another quick side hug.

"Come on Brandi, I'll show you the centerpieces I made for the retreat."

I follow her down a long hallway that leads to her station. While we walk, I relax at the sound of buzzing needles and Good Charlotte blasting through the shop's speakers. The atmosphere contains a busy calm that gets under your skin. It's hypnotic and I surrender to the vibe. I don't know how anyone leaves here without doing whatever Daphne wants you to do. She can talk me into anything, like hosting our annual book club retreat, but I draw the line at getting a tattoo.

Her first attempt to ink me was fifteen years ago, while we were pledging Rho Beta Chi and simultaneously drooling over Mr. Darcy in our shared English Literature classes. Neither one of us was an English major. I studied Political Science and Daphne studied graphic arts. We both fed our love of reading by sneaking English Literature classes in our schedule as electives.

At the time, I was six feet deep inside the grave of a break-up from my cheating ass fiancé, and Ciara was away studying abroad in France. Daphne was dreaming of art school while acclimating to the liberal arts institution her parents wanted her to attend. Somehow, we both knew that Austen would make it all better. Daphne suggested a tattoo that said, fuck men to heal my pain. I was tempted, but ultimately declined. Still, we became fast friends.

Honestly, the two of us have little else in common besides our love of community service and books. Lord knows I can't stand her taste in music or clothes. While she hates my penchant for Hermes and Louis Vuitton. But, for us that's enough. We aren't besties by any means; but we're there for each other when needed.

Besides, my best friend is Riddick Kruger, and he's irreplaceable.

Irreplaceable and sexy, with tattoos I'm too square to get, covering his strong back and chest.

Locally, he's a known sex God. I won't call him a man-whore, but Riddick loves the ladies, and Lord, do the ladies love him. Riddick's six feet and four inches of muscle and forever-tanned ivory skin has a lot to do with the copious amount of sex thrown his way. While I on the other hand haven't had sex in almost two decades. A fact that Ciara finds appalling, but I really don't care.

Sex is too risky. Before you know it, you're in love and throwing away your dreams because some man asks you to marry him and then betrays your trust in the worst way possible. Then you're trapped inside a small town and the decisions he made for you.

But I digress.

Despite my self-imposed celibacy, I crave Riddick. Right now, I'm obsessing over the fact that Daphne laid a lot of the ink on Riddick's incredible body. I'm jealous that she's had her hands on his naked skin, while I only dream about it. My hands slightly clench until Daphne touches my arm and redirects my thoughts.

"Brandi, since Ciara is busy, and this is no longer a simple pickup of table decorations. Why don't you finally let me give you an itty-bitty tattoo?" Daphne brings her thumb and index together for effect. "You know, somewhere discreet."

I make a big show of sighing. "My skin is too dark and lovely for tattoos. The vibrant colors swirling over your porcelain skin will never show up on mine."

Daphne narrows her eyes while she sips what I'm sure is her

tenth cup of tea today. She hates coffee, which is a mortal sin in my book. Java runs through my veins 24/7.

"Bullshit," she puffs out after swallowing a mouthful of tea. "My team and I are the best artists on the east coast. We carry ink for every possible skin tone. Plus, no one rocks a tattoo like a beautiful Black woman. Look at your sister! Her art is sexy as hell. You're doing the world a disservice by not allowing my needle to create on your beautiful canvas."

She pouts and points at me teasingly. "Just admit that you're wound too tight to allow a tattoo on your flawless skin. It's a shame though, because I think you would look fierce walking into courtrooms with a little ink peeking through all those cream silk blouses you wear."

I roll my eyes and shake my head.

"I won't look fierce. I'll look unprofessional. Something you and Ciara never have to worry about."

I drop my Louis Vuitton briefcase on the floor and lean against a set of cabinets in Daphne's booth to take in her shop. Every time I step inside, I sense her pride. She made her dream of owning a tattoo shop a reality, and that's impressive. As smart as Daphne is, I'm sure her parents had different plans for her. But this shop brings out the best in my shy sorority sister.

I've gone to enough book club meetings at Daphne's house to know she's not the most organized. Her house is clean, but chaotic. It would drive me nuts. In my home, everything has its place, and it's rarely out of it. Daphne visited a few times and declared me neurotic.

But the Ministry of Ink runs like a well-oiled machine. Not one needle or tube of ink is out of place. This is where her heart is. The shop is beautiful, light, and airy. There's framed art on the walls from every artist that works here. My favorite pieces are Daphne's. She paints renditions of her favorite books. They're priceless.

"Daphne, I'm not wound too tight. I'm a lawyer in a very conservative state. We can't all wear two beautiful sleeves of color to work every day. Now enough about the tattoo I'll never get. Do we have everything we need for the book club retreat? I finished this month's book late last night. It was hot with a capital H."

Daphne takes a seat in her client chair and nods. "It was! *Craving a King*, seriously had this punk rock loving tattoo artist looking up flights to Accra." Daphne swivels in the chair and closes her eyes with a dreamy look. "I need a man as sexy and powerful as King Kofi Ajyei. I mean, he lived in a mansion inside a forest, for Christ's sake! That's the dream. Louise Lennox really knows how to transport you to whatever place she's writing about."

"I agree. Between the steamy sex scenes and angst, I'm sure everyone will have something interesting to share about the read. Have you heard from everyone? Are they all coming down for homecoming and our retreat? Have you received all the RSVPs? You know our catering count must be exact!"

Daphne smiles. She's used to my exacting behavior and manages me well. "Calm down Brandi. You know the Meet Cute Book Club never misses an annual retreat or homecoming. All members will be present and accounted for."

The book club was our idea during my sophomore year at Abbott Ridge College. Daphne and I found ourselves at the local coffee shop, Books and Beans most Friday nights, happily reading a romance novel and drinking coffee. Neither one of us was much for the dating scene, and it was a natural progression from our class discussions.

One conversation led to another and soon we were swapping book recommendations. Once we pledged Rho Beta Chi, we found out a lot of our sisters loved romance novels too, so we made it official and started the book club. It's been going strong for fifteen years, and every time there's a new Rush, we open membership to the book club for a new sister or two. Early on, Ciara called our book club elitist and exclusionary. So, we opened it up. Any Rho Beta Chi member can sponsor a member whether they are in the sorority or not, and now we have an intimate, but more diverse membership.

Ciara still didn't join. She hates "joining" things.

Currently, there are eight core members and almost thirty auxiliary members. We usually meet online since we live all over the world. But once a year during homecoming weekend, we come together for our annual retreat. This year the group tapped Daphne and me to plan it. It's been a blast.

"OK, great. I'll be happy to see everyone. I will confirm the food for Sunday's meeting and brunch tomorrow. Picking up decorations from you and confirming the guest list were the last things on my list. Do you think Xavier or Glen can bring those boxes of decorations out to my car?"

Daphne nods and pulls out her phone to shoot a text. I'm sure her fellow artists don't want to be interrupted right now, but those boxes won't carry themselves. I also pick up my phone to shoot Ciara a text, but she beat me to it. *She's leaving with Seth.* I shake my head and remind her to be careful. But I'm not too worried since Daphne vouched for him.

I step away from the cabinets and take a deep breath. With the book club meeting details taken care of, I can focus on the true highlight of my homecoming weekend-the alumni step show.

"Daphne, are you coming to the step show tonight? Catherine and I are performing. It's going to be legendary!"

She shakes her head and frowns. "Sorry, I'll have to miss it. I have a back tattoo coming in at six. I doubt I'll be done in time. But I'll watch the recording. I know it will end up on your Instagram reels before the weekend is over."

I laugh and nod. *She's right.*

Daphne was never all that interested in the sorority extra-curricular activities. She joined to make her mom happy and to be of service to the community. The parties and step shows were never her jam. I reach over to give her a hug and she squeezes me tight. Her hugs are the best. When I pull back, I see a teasing sparkle in her eye.

"Is Riddick coming down from Raleigh to see you perform this weekend?"

Nope, my best friend is missing in action, and I do not know why.

Daphne swears Riddick, and I are secret lovers. I continually tell her we're only friends. She never takes my protests seriously.

To be honest, neither do I.

Sometimes, I wonder what it would be like to have a love life of my own. *To have Riddick...*

Then the slap of betrayal I felt the last time I fell in love strengthens my resolve to stay single and celibate. Lust clouds your judgment and can leave you inside a life you never designed for yourself.

I'm convinced Happily Ever After only happens in the books we read. Reality has proven to me it's nowhere near as nice as the endings I read every night before I go to bed.

Staying out of romantic liaisons is the only way to keep control of my life. *That and counting calories.*

Shaking off terrible memories, I huff and smooth my hair back from my face. "No, Riddick will not be coming. *But I wish he was.* He's staying in Raleigh to work on the newest restaurant he opened last month, *Busu.*"

Daphne pouts and reaches out to rub my arm. "I'm sorry hun. I know how much you look forward to his visits. He hasn't even visited his local bar, The Fall Line much this year. I heard one of his trusted managers is running it."

I scoff. "I'll survive. It's not like he's my man or anything. We're just friends."

She walks me through the shop and to the exit. "Mmm-hmm I know. I also know that almost two decades of close friendship is practically a marriage with no sex. You two are inseparable. Just jump each other's bones already and make it official."

"Daphne!" I half shout, before lowering my voice. "I am not jumping Riddick's bones. We are too important to each other for that." I shake my head. "I've got to go."

I blow her a kiss and push the door open. Wanting to leave her on a positive note, I look over my shoulder and shout. "I'll see you Sunday!"

She chuckles and waves goodbye.

Daphne thinks I'm in denial about Riddick. But I know better. I'm not in denial, I just know nothing good can come from Riddick and me having sex. He's always had a harem of women following him around to do whatever he pleases, and from what I hear, my bestie has some pretty dominant proclivities in bed.

A Submissive, I am not.

If I ever jumped back into the dating game, *and that's a big if;* I sure wouldn't start with a lothario like Riddick Kruger. I wouldn't survive it.

It's not like he wants me anyway...

Chapter 2

No Mercy
Riddick

I WANT to have sex with my best friend.

Lately, Brandi Armstrong takes up every thought crossing my mind. I don't know how or when it got this bad. We've been best friends for almost twenty years, and I spent most of them oblivious to her charms and my feelings.

Maybe not oblivious, but I certainly was not this infatuated.

Everything changed last year at the Abbott Ridge Inn's annual New Year's Party. Brandi and I attend every year to ring in the New Year together. At midnight, it's my duty to place a chaste kiss on her sweet lips and scream Happy New Year. We've performed that same ritual *Every. Fucking. Year.* But last year, the tight line of control I held concerning her snapped.

Before that night, all I felt towards Brandi was a strong sense of loyalty and devotion. I adored her in a nonthreatening way. My touches were benign. My words were benevolent and never carnal. That's what Brandi wanted, so that's what I gave her. From the moment we met, she threw up a wall of celibacy so high, no man attempted to climb it. *Not even me.*

Maybe my feelings changed because I turned 35 the day before the party or maybe because she looked like a damn goddess in the little champagne sequined dress she wore. No matter, I knew if I kissed her at midnight, I'd never stop. I would claim her delicious little mouth for all the world to see and never let go until she was a breathless puddle of need and want. I wanted her like I wanted nothing or anyone else before. So, I hugged her and bypassed her lips all together.

When I saw the hurt and confusion on her face, I knew I had to tell her the truth. So, I did.

The next time I kiss your lips; you're mine.

She stared at me with a dazed look and absently touched her lips for a moment. Then she snapped out of it and laughed.

She. Laughed.

The woman laughed until tears wet her eyes and she told me to stop being silly. Then she joked that I probably didn't kiss her because her breath stinks. That's when I knew I couldn't only be her friend anymore.

I will have all of her. I must make her see me differently.

Only thing is, I did not know how to do that with Brandi.

I'm dominant. Not in a hardcore BDSM kind of way, even though I don't mind a bit of kink. I'm talking about presence. I overwhelm women with fiery touches and dirty words. I make sinful promises and indulge in their wildest desires. In the past, I've only dealt with women who were free in their sexuality and knew exactly what they wanted from me. They were also just as clear as what they wouldn't get from me-*love*.

My modus operandi won't work with Brandi. She's way to wound up to respond to my methods. Sexually, she'll never relax long enough to let me take the lead. She also won't let me pull the *I don't do relationships and love* crap with her. Shit, I wouldn't want her to. *She's special.*

I'm at a loss on how to proceed because I don't know how to be anyone else but myself. I don't know how to be the loving and loyal boyfriend-I've never had to be one before. I work all the time. My restaurants keep me extremely busy, and she deserves more than my leftover minutes.

This year, I've hidden from her like a coward. It hurts too

much to be around her. I lose myself in her jet-black eyes and drown in her smile. Her dark skin is an aphrodisiac and reminds me of the jet-black beaches of Martinique. Her hair: usually in a large curly afro or pressed straight down to hang to her ass, beckons me to wrap my fist around a handful of it and dive into her sweet pussy.

Despite my self-imposed exile, we talk almost every day, because I need to know she's OK. Otherwise, I'll worry myself to death. I only avoided her physical presence like the plague because I knew the moment she was in touching range; I'd take her in my arms.

Now, it's ten months later and I'm slowly losing my shit. I'm sitting in my newest restaurant at the bar waiting for a business associate and all I'm thinking about is Brandi's sweet smell. She always smells like peaches and honey.

Damn. I need her. If I jerk off any harder to dirty fantasies of her riding my cock, it just might fall off. I don't only want her in my life; I want her in my bed. That's where she'll be as soon as I figure out how the fuck to tell her all this without scaring her. Brandi Armstrong has no desire to fall in love or onto my dick.

That much I know.

I down another drink before I finally eye my line brother Byron Logan walking in.

He's late.

The man is an annoying arrogant prick. I tolerate him because he's my fraternity brother. He's also a real estate investment guru that helps make me a lot of money.

I started investing with Byron years ago and he's helped me secure a lot of the properties my restaurants sit on. The man knows how to make a buck. My father taught me that sometimes you need a man like that around.

My restaurants are my pride and joy. I have two in Atlanta, two in Houston, and two in Miami. I even have a small restaurant and wine bar in Abbott Ridge. It was my first establishment and it's simple and good like the town. The Fall Line reminds me of my college days with Brandi. Now I want to open something even bigger and more authentic to the area in Abbott Ridge.

I create worldwide retreats with food. Each of my restaurant pairings in a location represents cities that pair together in the world. In Miami, for example, the restaurants represent Havana and San Juan. The décor is glamorous and authentic to the region being celebrated. The food and wine lists are always native to the countries. All six of my establishments are extremely popular, with waiting lists over six months long. They've made me a very rich man. In Abbott Ridge, I think a farm to table masterpiece with an accompanying vineyard would give the town a jolt of energy. I just need to find the space.

Byron called and asked to meet today. He claims he's found the perfect property for me to create my Abbott Ridge dream. I agreed to meet, because I've wanted to do this for a while, and I know Brandi will approve if I don't use a distressed farm. She loves her hometown like I love my hometown of Cape Town, South Africa. It's a part of her and she longs to see it grow and develop. I feel like this restaurant will bring us together. It will force the proximity we've been missing the last few years while I opened restaurants all over the southeast.

"Frat," Byron grins and I stand to give him some dap and a strong pat on the back. My wait for him at the bar was strategic because I don't want to stay long. If we were in the dining area or even my office, he would try to twist my arm to stay for dinner. With Byron, I keep everything strictly business.

He slides onto the stool next to me and I motion for the bartender. I force a smile. "What you drinking Frat?"

In our organization, your fraternity brother, or frat, is like a blood brother. Family, in the deepest sense of the word. Sometimes, the men don't rise to the title. With Byron, I'm still trying to figure out if that's the case.

He holds out his hands. "Just water for me. I don't put any poison into this temple. It's too valuable."

He throws me a haughty look and I eye the motherfucker right back. He's so full of shit. The man eats triple cheeseburgers for breakfast. While I adhere to a strict Paleo diet with the occasional tumbler of cognac. *I loathe hypocrites.*

It's obvious he was the man women chased when he was younger. He's tall, shorter than me, but still a formidable 6'3. He's light skinned and pretty, as Brandi's late grandmother would say. However, he's also about 25 pounds overweight and graying early at his temples.

He was the quarterback of his high school football team, a rich kid, and smart as shit. He was no doubt Abbott Ridge's golden boy. Whenever I ask Brandi about him, she confirms the latter. Everyone in town thought the sun rose and sat on his ass. It's obvious Brandi wasn't too fond of him.

I toss the rest of my drink back and shrug. "Suit yourself. Tell me about this land you've found. I'm eager to get started."

His mouth cracks into a slick grin. The look is treacherous. He's about to say some bullshit. *Damn, I've wasted my time.* I'll never agree to whatever has him smiling like the damn Cheshire cat.

This has happened before. Sometimes Byron picks properties that prey on the weak or are shady and I decline. He knows I'll never go for it, but he tries, anyway. I swear if he wasn't my frat-*and so good at securing investors*-I'd stop working with him all together. Lately, he's kept the dealings clean to avoid my wrath. Today, though, it looks like he's bringing bullshit. *Whatever, I'm here now.*

He leans over and whispers like what he's saying is top secret. "This is the largest score in North Carolina Frat. We're going to buy Edenton Shores, lock, stock, and barrel and then you can have not only the restaurant you've always talked about, but a vineyard too.

I stare, trying to figure out what his game is. He must be out of his damn mind. Edenton Shores is Brandi's family farm. It's been in her family for over 150 years. Her grandfather, Ellis Armstrong III, would rather die than let some slimy asshole like Byron buy it from up under him and turn it into one of his ventures. *Like my restaurants.*

Brandi's goal in life is to ensure every Black farmer in North Carolina keeps ownership of their farms and not be forced to sell because of bad loans. That's the main reason I stay away from indebted farmlands when I go into deals with Byron. The farms must be on the up and up, with owners that are ready to sell. I won't buy from anyone backed into a financial corner. Brandi would never forgive me if I did. She hates that I work with Byron at all, but I tease her off by saying that she can't be my only friend.

All that aside, I seriously doubt anyone is buying Edenton Shores. Brandi fights Byron in court at least once a year over his scheming and she always wins.

This sounds personal.

Why would he go after her family's land, and how the hell did they even come up on his radar? Is the farm in trouble? I keep my cool so I can see what he's up to, because I know one thing for sure: if it sounds like he's going to hurt Brandi-I'll destroy him.

I clear my throat. "I'm surprised the family agreed to sell. Ellis Armstrong hates developers."

He laughs. "Brandi Armstrong hates developers. Don't play games with me Riddick, I know you've had your nose wide open for Brandi for the better part of seventeen years. You two deeming each other best friends."

The way he sneers the last words tells me this is indeed personal. But I don't know why. They fight in courtrooms-but that's business. *Isn't it?* My hackles are up, but I continue to listen while he continues to dig his grave.

"You think because you two are close that you know everything about her and her family? Well, I can tell you that you don't. I've done my due diligence and I know for a fact that Edenton Shores is underwater. It has been for a while. Her cousin Mae reached out to me. She wants to see what I can do to help set her family up for life. The farm is draining them financially dry. Their grandfather is getting older; he won't be here forever. Mae and Darius have the rest of their lives and a daughter to think about. Ciara will eventually want her cut too. So, I made them an offer they can't refuse. Everyone wins."

Except Brandi. This will crush her.

I shake my head at the slimy piece of shit sitting across from me. He's sitting in my restaurant talking about taking something from Brandi. Mae is always at odds with Brandi and Ciara about the fate of Edenton Shores, but I never thought she'd go this far. She must be tired of running the farm and, according to Byron, it's losing money. *I'll have to check his facts.*

Either way, Brandi is going to eat Byron's heart for lunch and then his ass for dinner over this. I will enjoy watching the carnage.

Before facing my frat brother, I gesture for another drink. "I understand money motivates Mae, but isn't Edenton Shores heir land? All Ellis' descendants would have to agree to sell. Given what Brandi does for a living and how much she loves Edenton Shores, I can't imagine she's going to give up an inch of that land for development."

Byron stiffens and knocks his water back. No doubt now wishing it was something stronger. "Whatever. That bitch will do whatever her family wants her to, because she doesn't want to farm. Brandi wants to grandstand and make speeches all over North Carolina, pretending to care about Black farmers. She was the same way in high school. She's never done a hard day's work to till the soil she waxes so poetically about in the courtroom."

I forgot they went to high school together.

I squeeze my glass so hard I'm afraid it might shatter. He's never talked about Brandi with so much venom, and I don't like it. He called her a bitch, and that's enough to cause me to throat punch him until he's gasping for breath. He knows how close Brandi and I are, and he's trying to rile me up. *I just don't know why.* But it doesn't matter because doit worked.

"If I were you, Byron, I'd watch my words." I lace my voice

with steel. "You're talking about my best friend; someone I love and respect above most people in my life. One thing she is not and never will be is a female dog. Don't disrespect her again, or I will disrespect you with my fist. Am I clear?"

Byron throws me a hard stare. He's got something to say, but he knows to choose his words carefully. I'll fuck him up right here in my restaurant. I don't give a damn.

When he rubs the back of his neck and laughs; I'm a bit thrown. I stare at him with murder in my eyes, and he clears his throat. "You know what your problem is, Riddick. You think Brandi's yours. She's not yours and she'll be no one's again."

He scoots his stool closer, encroaching my space. My fists clench and unclench in my lap. "You want to know why? Because she was mine." He waits for my reaction, but I don't give him one.

What. The. Fuck. What does he mean she was his?

I swallow down my surprise to let him continue. "Yeah, that's right. You can sit there and act like you're not in love with her, but everybody knows you are. Only I know why she won't let you see you neither hide, nor hair of that pussy."

He chuckles, signing his death warrant.

"It's because I owned that pussy seventeen years ago, when she was my fiancée. Every time your friend looks at me in court, she remembers I beat her pussy up every night and still would be if she hadn't fucked everything up. Now she can't stand the thought of being with no one else. She's still sweating me to this day, and you know one thing I can't stand is a thirsty bitch."

My ears ring with a whooshing sound and red flashes before my eyes. I know what I'm going to do and I'm helpless to stop it. This rat is talking about the woman I love, and I won't have it. Before he takes another breath, I step off my stool and grab him by his shirt to throw him against the bar. I lean over and wrap my hand around his neck until my face almost touches his. My breathing is only a rumbled roar. The bar clears out around me, and the few that dare to remain watch like it's is prime time television.

"What the fuck did you say about Brandi?" He coughs and sputters. The spittle flying everywhere when he tries to talk. But I could not care less.

His arms flail, and he turns beet red. "Man, get off me! I'll sue your White ass for assault!'

I laugh and lick my lips. "Oh, now let's not bring my race into this Byron. You don't really want to sue me, because you know whether I'm black, green or purple; I can buy and sell your slimy ass two or three times over. I'll have you tied up in court for the rest of your pathetic life. You'll be so bogged down with legal fees that you won't be able to close one fucking deal."

"Now, let me tell you what's going to happen. You're gonna stay the hell away from Brandi, her family, and their land. If I think for one second that you're doing anything underhanded that could hurt Brandi, I will end you. I hope you understand… Frat."

I spit the last words at him before throwing him back against the bar. He coughs, trying to catch his breath. When he can speak, his words are as weak as he is.

"Riddick, you're so fucked. We're done! I hope that b…" He pauses. "I hope Brandi is worth it. Because we're never doing business again, and I'll make sure you never open another restaurant here in Abbott Ridge. My family owns this town and the council."

I'm glad he self-corrected before he called Brandi out of her name again. I'd hate to really beat his ass. I have no problem breaking every bone in his body, but I'd rather not spill blood on my floors. *I just opened this restaurant.* Regardless, next time he talks crazy about Brandi will be the last time he speaks. I smirk and move close enough to him to whisper. I relish in his stiffened posture. *He should be scared.*

"Save the drama Byron. Your family owns the Abbott Ridge the public sees, but we both know who really runs this town. I'm sure my friend Seth and the Black Knights would love to know what you've been up to on their turf. He can find me an uncompromised property to open my restaurant on. You are dismissed."

He looks shocked. He doesn't know that I know his family duped many families out of their holdings. Or that they've bought seats on the city council. I always thoroughly vet my business partners, whether they're my frat brother or not. He also doesn't know that the head of the Black Knights Motorcycle Club, Seth Canton, owes me a favor. I catered his mama's repast when she died ten years ago for free. Back then, he didn't have two nickels to rub together. I did it because his mama was a good woman and he asked. He promised he would pay me back one day. I never needed him to, but I might need his influence now.

Byron straightens up and rubs his neck. *I hope it hurts.*

"I cut Brandi loose all those years ago because she was holding me back. It looks like she's doing the same thing to you. Don't come crawling back to me when she finally cuts you off. She's damn near crazy now." He backs away, and the further he gets away from me, his courage builds. "I will buy Edenton Shores, because the rest of her family wants to sell. Even her sister Ciara is considering it. You just won't have the privilege of opening your restaurant on it-someone else will."

He storms out of my restaurant and knocks a chair over on his way out. I count to ten, so I don't go after him and bash his head into the side of the stupid G Wagon he drives. *I hate oversized gas guzzling machines.*

I nod to the bartender to clean up the mess I made while choking the shit out of Byron. Then I sit with the information I just learned about Byron and Brandi and shake my head in disappointment and mild rage.

Brandi never told me she was engaged, let alone to that fool. No wonder she hates him with a singular passion. She knows that Byron and me pledged together, but she also knows I can't really stand his simple ass.

Why didn't she tell me, and what happened?

Now her hesitancy towards relationships makes more sense. The broken heart she had when I first met her all those years ago and the way she keeps her heart on lockdown is all because of Byron.

Something from the story is missing. He had to have done something heinous. I won't tell Brandi I know yet, because if she wanted me to know she would have told me. Eventually it will all come out, but for now, none of that's important. But I'd put money on the fact that he broke her, and that alone makes me want to go find him right now and beat him to a bloody pulp.

Today, I'll push all that aside because I need to warn Brandi.

She doesn't know this fool is coming for her legacy.

Chapter 3

No Patience

Brandi

MY DAY JUST GOT BETTER.

I slide into the driver's seat and Riddick's name flashes across my electric Audi Q5's LCD Dash. It's crazy. Daphne and me were just talking about him and now he's calling. I answer and slowly back out of the Ministry of Ink's parking lot.

"And to what do I owe this honor, Mr. Kruger? I haven't heard from you in over a week! You must need something."

He laughs and my insides melt. No one laughs like Riddick Kruger. His sexy chuckle is a deep baritone filled rumble, and it holds a hint of danger and lust. The latter has a lot to do with his South African Accent. He sounds like a mix of Liam Hemsworth, Prince Harry, and Idris Elba. It's the hottest sound on earth,

"I always need you, Kitten. Did you miss me?"

I always miss you.

Riddick has called me kitten for as long as I've known him. It started as a joke. When we met, I kept two illegal kittens in my dorm room and the Resident Hall Director tried to make me get rid of them. But I lived with animals my entire life and I would not stop because of some stupid college dorm rules. I was coming out of my disaster of a relationship with Byron, and the kittens were my emotional support animals.

Riddick stuck up for me at the dorm council meeting. He was on the housing panel because he was an RA. Just when I thought I'd lost my case, this man with a delicious accent stood up and defended me like I was his. He went on about the right to mental health support and mentioned that he ran my floor and has had no complaints.

After the meeting, I went to thank him, and he gave me tips on how to continue to keep the kittens unheard and unseen. He's called me kitten ever since. How he's turned such a simple word into the sexiest one on earth, I'll never know. He pulls me apart piece by piece whenever he uses it.

"No! I didn't miss you." I answer too quickly.

Get it together Brandi!

"Hmmm," Riddick hums. "It sounds like you did."

I search for a witty comeback. "How can I miss a bugaboo that only calls when he needs something?"

Riddick laughs. "I see, well if you're going to call me names, I will not tell you the information I have on your favorite foe, Byron Logan."

Bastard. My douchebag of an ex is my sworn enemy and Riddick doesn't even know the half of why, but I'd rather die than tell him about that stupid chapter of my life.

"OK Kruger, spill it."

I hear his sardonic smile over the phone. "Of course, he came into the restaurant talking big shit like he always does about our newest potential venture. You know Byron."

I do know Byron. That's why I take great pleasure whenever I knock him down a peg or two in court. He's the most dishonorable real estate lawyer to walk the earth. But he is also Riddick's line brother. Byron has helped Riddick secure most of the properties his six restaurants sit on. I try to respect the fact they're friends on some level. But that doesn't mean I have to like him. He's a cheating creep that broke my heart.

I've never told Riddick how we're connected because I never wanted to expose him to my drama. It's embarrassing. What happened between Byron, and I was the lowest point of my life. I was weak and out of control. Riddick doesn't want to know that part of me. I knew Byron would never tell him because he was the villain in that story. Byron Logan isn't talking about himself unless he's bragging or showing himself in the best light. What he did to my family, and I was unforgivable.

Riddick continues, "He has his eyes on Edenton Shores. He offered me first dibs on the property, since I want to open an Abbott Ridge location. Of course, I declined, but he says your family is ready to sell."

"The fuck they are," I seethe. "My grandfather would never sell our land to someone as sleazy as Byron Logan. I know shit can't be that bad on the farm."

Can it? Work has kept me busy. I haven't visited the farm in a while. If anything was truly wrong, I know my grandfather would call me. He'd rather die than sell to Byron. He hates him and the Logans as much as I do.

Riddick's long pause rattles me. He always delivers bad news like I'm made of glass. One minor nervous breakdown my sophomore year and I'm forever "fragile" in his eyes.

"Kitten, he didn't speak to your grandfather." He sighs and pauses again. I provide the wait time he needs, trusting he'll get there.

"He's been speaking with your cousin Mae."

Fuckity, fuck, fuck!

"What!" I yell into the car. *This time she's gone too far.* "Is she crazy?"

She's always up to some sneaky backhanded shit.

"Riddick, you know as well as I do that she's been financially draining the farm dry for the past ten years. I don't know what the hell her problem is, but this time, we're gonna fight!"

She's due for a meeting with my foot up her ass.

Riddick produces another sexy chuckle and for a moment, I forget why I'm mad. "Calm down Kitten. I'm sure Mae has an explanation. Plus, how do we even know what Byron said about

Mae is true? He could attempt to squeeze your family on his own. There's no need for violence."

I want to rage at him for being so stupid and trusting. Then I remember he has no clue how low Mae really can go. *Hopefully, he'll never find out.*

"Pfft. The hell there isn't. She's going to tell me exactly what's going on and what she's up to, or I'm going to beat it out of her treacherous behind. She's not selling our family's legacy up from under us. And if she doesn't listen to me, I'll send Ciara. And we both know Mae doesn't want that drama."

Ciara's crazy as hell. I may have a temper. But she goes nuclear with Mae. She's been a thorn in our side for years.

I make a U-turn in the middle of the road; knowing it's reckless, but I don't care. *Plus, nothing handles like an Audi.* Anger rips through my body like a five-alarm fire.

"I'm heading over there right now."

"Wait... What?" Riddick barks. His sexy chuckle is gone and replaced by his high-handed friend-*the bark.* "Brandilyn Julene Armstrong, you can't go over there half-cocked. It's just going to make things worse. Look, it's Byron you're mad at, not Mae."

I snort. If only he knew. "Nope, I promise you, it's Mae. I expect Byron to be an idiot. She should know better."

Riddick Sighs. "Brandi, she's your grandfather's legal and financial representative. He trusts her. She practically runs that farm. If what Byron says is true, you need her on your side. Why don't you pause and try to see what's going on at Edenton Shores from her point of view? Maybe the farm is having some trouble. Better yet, just wait until I can come into town and I'll go with you. You should approach this with a level head."

I roll my eyes. Riddick is always talking that cooler heads prevail bullshit. I haven't seen him in person for the better part of a year, and now he wants to volunteer to come down here to keep me in line? *Fuck. That.* Sometimes you need to fight. He doesn't know Mae like I do. She will do anything for a quick payday. He doesn't know about the extra mortgages she's put on the property for supposed repairs. Ain't shit repaired on that farm, but Mae's new tits.

"No, Riddick. I'm going right now!'

He releases a loud breath. "Don't you have the step show tonight? You can't miss that. If you wait a few days, I can come up there and help you smooth things over."

"Nope, I've got plenty of time. And if you came to Home-coming to watch me show these young neophytes, I've still got it; you would already be here, wouldn't you? So, whose fault is that? Also, why are you defending Mae!"

He exhales and chuckles. "I'm not defending Mae, Brandi. All I'm saying is that she may have good reason to seek out Byron. We don't know what the financial situation on the farm is. We may not know what Edenton Shores needs."

I narrow my eyes and squeeze my fists around the steering wheel. "One thing it doesn't need is to be sold and chopped up to create some restaurant or tourist destination. Which is exactly the business Byron, and you, I might add are in. It's a farm, one of the few working Black farms left in the nation, and I intend it to stay that way. Hopefully, you do too."

He mumbles something under his breath. Probably a nice string of curse words, not that he'd ever let me hear them. I smirk. "That's low Kitten. You know I don't buy distressed properties, and I don't like you insinuating that I would have designs on Edenton Shores. Don't you know I'd rather die than hurt you? Is that not clear in every fucking word I say to you?"

Whoa. OK, he did let me hear that one. *He's mad.*

"Riddick, I'm sorry. You know Mae makes me crazy. I know you would never hurt me that way. Look, the show is in four hours. I'm just going to make a quick stop at Edenton Shores and put a stop to her scheming before it takes flight; then I'll be on my way. If she knows I know what she's up to, she'll back off."

Riddick scoffs. "Yeah right. Back off isn't exactly in Mae's vocabulary. That's one character trait you two have in common."

I ignore the jab because I don't have time to fight with him right now. I need to save all my energy for Mae. "Regardless Riddick, thanks for the heads up. You always look out and give me what I need."

Wait. That sounded bizarrely intimate.

Riddick hums. "It's my pleasure to give you what you need, but you don't need another reason to fight Mae. I should have kept this information to myself until I knew more."

Whatever. He did exactly what he should have done. Consequences be damned. He waits a while before releasing a frustrated breath.

"Just be careful and try to listen to Mae, Kitten. OK? Promise me?"

I bite my bottom lip and slam my turn signal up in frustration. "Yeah, OK, I promise. Look, I need to concentrate on the road. I'll call you later, OK?"

It's clear he doesn't want to hang up, but he knows when he's beat. He shouldn't have told me if he didn't want me to act. But he couldn't do that either, because he knows if I ever found out, he knew and didn't tell me I'd have his balls on a silver platter. Finally, he speaks.

"Alright, be safe. Call me afterwards."

"Got it. Bye Riddick!"

I hang up and gun my engine. I don't have a minute to lose. My righteous indignation is at an all-time high. If Mae knows what's good for her, she'll confess and drop the matter entirely. Knowing my cousin, the exact opposite will happen.

Good thing I still know how to kick some ass.

Chapter 4

No Family

Brandi

GOD, Grant me patience to deal with fools...

"Mae, why do you want to start your weekend off with my foot up your ass?"

One after the other, my 14 Karat diamond hoops hit the brown dirt separating the neat rows of my grandfather's cotton plants. It's mid-September, and I'm surprised someone has not harvested them. *Where are the workers?* The crop has been ready for weeks. Thankfully, their height is high enough to provide Mae and I excellent cover. It's best I whip her behind in private.

"You ain't finna do shit, you stuck-up witch!" She lunges for my hair, but I side-step her. She always goes for my hair... *so predictable.*

I come to my family's farm for quiet reflection; not to fight. The sight of the rolling green fields broken only by rows of my grandfather's beloved crops brings me peace of mind. I'm a lawyer, so I fight for a living, and I'm always defending someone's cause.

When I come to Edenton Shores, I just want to walk barefoot in the grass and reclaim my center of gravity- all while I enjoy these fields, our family's one hundred fifty-year-old white shingled farmhouse, and eat real farm to table food, such as my grandmother's turnip greens and her wine. She's gone, but her recipes, garden, and grape vines live on.

Today, I don't get to focus on any of those things. *I'm ready to fight.*

I tried to be civil. My cousin is doing business with my ex-fiancé, and I simply want to know why. Doesn't she know he's one of the sleaziest corporate real estate raiders in the state of North Carolina? *Of course, she does.*

I've dealt with Byron more times than I like to count in courtrooms from one side of the state to the other. His M.O. is to find farms in financial trouble, *back against the wall trouble,* and offer half of what their land is worth in cash. He convinces the cash-strapped families he's doing them a favor while the increasing pressure of foreclosure looms over them. Instead of investing in their generational dreams, he snuffs their dreams out. The farmers take what he gives because they are desperate.

Then he sells their farmland to commercial investors, *like Riddick,* or the same corporate farms that squeeze the livelihood out of the family farms. Those corporations have no conscience, and often belong to his family's business: Logan Agricultural Holdings. *It makes me sick.* Especially when he used to promise me, we would spend our lives fighting the kind of men he's now turned out to be.

My first encounter with him after our break-up was while I was at Duke Law. After he broke my heart, I avoided him like the plague he was. Third-year students volunteered for our favorite professor, Dr. Wayne's, community law clinic in Durham. He opened the clinic back in the eighties when he noted the lack of advocacy for local minority farmers. Predatory land schemes and corporate farms disproportionately affected them. I was shocked to see that Byron was on the wrong side of the first case I worked on.

Once I stepped foot into the legal side of things, I never left it. In my gut, I knew any of the farmers we helped could easily be my grandfather. One or two poor crops and he could be at the mercy of the gutless sharks taking land from families for pennies on the dollar.

Before my work with Dr. Wayne, my plan was to attend Duke for a fancy law degree and leave. I wanted to move to New York and practice corporate law. I wanted to run from the small town that held all my terrible memories. I planned to still volunteer and offer services to farmers for pro bono, but I needed to get out of Abbott Ridge for good. I desperately wanted to leave behind our small downtown with three stoplights, beautiful park square with dogwood and oak trees larger than life, and the green rolling hills of Abbott Ridge College. My prestigious law degree was supposed to be my ticket to a new life.

Instead, I fell in love with defending the environmental and farm rights of poor farmers in North Carolina. When I got back home to Abbott Ridge, I opened my advocacy center, and it's thriving. Root Rights Law Group is my pride and joy.

Imagine my surprise today when Riddick tipped me off. *I just can't believe Byron is in talks with my family about buying our farm.* That's low, even for him.

I know Byron didn't talk to Ellis Armstrong, the third. My grandfather would shoot him before he got to the gate. Nope, the lone culprit was my lovely and selfish cousin Mae.

The same cousin I caught Byron fucking behind the barn three months after we got engaged.

Her trifling ass would sell our family land from under us without a second thought. She always thought Edenton Shores was her private bank to drain and that any man was hers to take. When we were younger, she thought she was better than me, because she was exceptionally beautiful and she had a knack for working the land that kept us clothed, fed, and educated. I focused on my books. I wanted to learn how we could ensure we kept our land. The law could do that.

Even now she's standing with her hands on her hips, looking like she has a million other things to do than explain herself to me. After a beat, she crosses her arms and rolls her eyes.

"Girl, you ain't fittin' to do shit in that prissy white suit you're wearing. What is that, anyway? Silk? Who the fuck wears silk to a farm? It's eighty degrees and sticky out here! OH, that's right. You never come out here 'less you want to throw your money and those damn degrees around."

I'm going to knock her dirt-covered high yellow block off!

As kids, Mae Battle Armstrong could do no wrong. She won every beauty pageant she entered and charmed every adult that came her way. Her parents died in the same boating accident as Ciara and mine did. Our mothers were sisters. So, for a while, the three of us became sisters in grief.

At only one year apart, Mae and I were close, but competitive. Our grandfather called us Ebony and Ivory because we were always together and had totally different complexions. I am the same deep brown as the earth he farms, while Mae is the color of the churned butter grandma makes. I hated the comparison, but it tickled him, so it stuck. If he knew how long it took me to get over the colorism that plagues our community, maybe he would have stopped.

Mae got a pass on everything at school while I had to prove I was worthy of attention by studying harder and doing everything twice as good. If I heard one more adult tell me "I was pretty for a dark-skinned girl," I would have screamed. *But that's small-town North Carolina for you.* Instead, I focused on being the best at everything else and not letting Mae beat me in anything except farm work. That she could have. Our relationship became defined by a competition. I was determined she would never win. Through it all, I truly believed we still loved each other-bound by not just blood, but grief.

Then she fucked Byron, and shit was never the same.

"I come home!" I screech.

I hate sounding defensive, but she's hit a sore spot. Riddick warned me not to come to the farm emotional and half-cocked, but I didn't listen. I still hear his disapproving South African accent in my ear now… *Brandi, be careful and try to listen.*

You know what? Fuck him. I begged him to come to homecoming this weekend, but he swore he had too much work to do. If I didn't know he was also skipping the step show tonight, I would think he's full of shit. He's put me off all year about coming to Abbott Ridge. He's always working. But, if he's missing any part of homecoming, especially the step show, his restaurants must have him slammed.

Damn, I wish he was here.

I should calm down and try to see why Mae would make such a desperate move. However, at this moment, I am not interested in Mae's point-of-view. In my mind, she doesn't have one. *She never has.*

Mae wields power as our grandparents' caregiver with precision. She lives with them because she fucked around and got pregnant not long after fucking Byron. She latched onto the town fool and football star, Darius Luck. Mae was just as desperate to leave farm life behind as I was, but she couldn't.

She barely finished high school and Darius was supposed to go to the NFL. Now she's 36 and married to a man still crying over a bum knee. At least we got my baby cousin, Toya, out of the deal. She's a seventeen-year-old freshman at my alma mater, Abbottt Ridge College. My baby is a genius! She's pledging my sorority, Rho Beta Chi and crossing over this weekend. I couldn't be prouder of her.

My grandfather hates that Mae and I don't get along. He doesn't know that she slept with Byron. If it's up to me, he won't know until the good Lord calls him home and then Jesus can tell him. I'm not trying to protect Mae. I just don't want granddaddy going to jail. If he knew, I'm pretty sure he'd shoot Byron. It was hard enough convincing him not to get his shotgun Jeanie out when Byron broke off our engagement. Of course, I'm the one that broke it off after I found him naked and rolling around with Mae. All granddaddy knew is that Byron broke a promise to me, and to granddaddy, that was a sin punishable by death.

I step in and push my palms into Mae's chest. She stumbles backwards as I seethe. How dare she talk about my fashion sense?

"Mae, you're mad because you can't afford silk."

She doesn't react.

I push her again. This time, she glares back at me. She's mad. *Good, I want to fight.* I smirk.

"And the color is ivory. But you wouldn't know pearl from taupe because you're always in those same ugly ass black yoga pants and plaid shirt looking like Old McDonald had a fucking fashion mishap!"

Fire hits Mae's eyes and the next thing I know, we're rolling around on the ground like two teenagers. Except we're not teenagers. We are two grown women messing up my very expensive Celine suit.

Mae has about twenty pounds on me because she's never seen the inside of spin class and eats whatever the fuck she wants. I'm in better shape, but she's stronger than me. Plus, she's a mother. Unfortunately for me, women who have birthed babies have super powered strength.

I used to hope to one day become acquainted with that strength. Now that I'm thirty-five, I think that dream has died. I have no man to speak of and zero patience for dating. My biological clock sounds regular alarms, but all I focus on is winning my next case and saving more farms.

However, none of that is on my mind right now because I can't breathe. Mae has straddled and pinned me to the ground.

"Eat dirt Brandi!" she screams.

She's force feeding me the same soil we used to dig up together as kids. Mae, Ciara, and I were the three amigos. We thought nothing was cooler than planting flower bulbs and watching them bloom. That was as close to farm work as I got, but our garden was legendary. When Mae turned sixteen and discovered boys, she suddenly no longer had time to plant. That was the first time Ciara and I learned she was flaky as a buttered biscuit.

I turn my head back and forth to escape the assault, but Mae keeps at it. "What's the matter cousin, does this meal not fit your perfect 1500 calorie count? I swear you're a psycho. Who the hell eats the same number of calories every day!?"

What did she call me? She knows I hate to be called anything along those lines. I was diagnosed with an anxiety disorder after my break-up with Byron. It was the lowest point in my life. My life felt so out of control that I took solace in controlling what I eat with exacting standards. I never knocked the habit, but that does not make me a psycho. Shit, it just makes me slim.

Mae knows all of this, but she's never given a damn. She thought what she did was no big deal back then. My sweet cousin claims she didn't know we were that serious, and she's taken no responsibility for fucking Byron. She lacks accountability. Her words are a low hurtful blow, and she's going to pay for them.

I get my hands free and punch her in the chest. She coughs and flies backwards.

I take advantage and jump on top of her. Just when I reach for some dirt to give her a piece of her own medicine, I feel myself being lifted into the air. I know who it is without looking.

The fool.

"Now ladies, let's stop all this doggoned foolishness. What the hell are all y'all fighting over anyhow?" Darius is holding me by my stomach, but I'm kicking like a banshee and he finally has to drop me. I immediately get back up and lunge at Mae, but Darius is quicker than me. He picks her up off the ground and tosses her over his shoulder.

"Nah Brandi. I can't let you beat up my wife."

"She would not beat me!" Mae screeches from over his shoulder.

He shakes his head. "Babe, from what I saw, it wasn't looking too good."

I glare at her and blow the hair out of my face. Two hours at a Dominican salon to get this curly mop on my head pressed for the alumni homecoming step show tonight and I'm already sweating it out. I'm going to have to put some heat to these edges before I hit the stage, which will take time I don't have.

Damn, I really should have listened to Riddick and waited.

Brushing the dirt off my now stained pants, I collect myself before continuing. "Mae, you know good and well that once I was on top of you, it was a wrap. Your ass was grass!"

She tries to push off Darius to jump down and come at me, but it's no use. He swats her butt and I swear I hear her moan. I roll my eyes and he smirks. When she finally calms down, he sets her on her feet, and we face each other like two storm clouds ready to rain down on someone's head. Darius sighs and turns his focus back to me.

"Brandi, is this about us selling Edenton Shores?"

I laugh. "No, this is about y'all not selling Edenton Shores."

"You can't control everyone and this farm, Brandi." Mae mettles the words out between her panting breaths. "You're not the fucking queen of Edenton Shores, no matter how far that stick is up your ass!"

"I'm not trying to control anyone. I'm trying to protect our family. Not that you give a damn about that! You've never given a damn about anyone or anything but yourself. Your loyalty is to Mae and what Mae needs, but I'm over catching consequences for your selfish actions. You ruined my life once. You won't do it again by stealing something as important as the farm away from me... away from us!"

My words are full of venom, and immediately I regret them. It's been over seventeen years, but I still can't forgive her. I know that's a problem. But it's too late. Mae flinches, and like me, she won't bow. *That's truly the one thing we have in common.* She'd rather die than back down or admit I hurt her. She lunges forward, but Darius stops her with one look and a mild shake of his head before he turns to me and lifts his hands in mock surrender.

"Look Brandi. No one is going to do anything without the whole family on board. There's nothing wrong with Mae and I talking to Mr. Logan about possibilities and options. When was the last time you looked at the farm balance sheets?" I pause and glance away. "Right, because you don't live here; Mae, your grandfather and I do. We are bleeding money and if we don't do something soon, we will lose the farm either way. At least this way, we can work with someone who knows our family and will give us a good deal-despite the past."

Mae crosses her arms across her artificially perky chest and rolls her eyes. "Exactly. Your high and mighty ass lives across town in a mansion while we're over here trying to make ends meet. At least Byron is trying to help."

I roll my eyes and brush the dirt off my suit. "Cry me a river Mae. No one told you to keep convincing grandfather to take loans out against the farm to fund your get rich quick schemes. It goes back further than that. No one told you to drop out of school, fuck my fiancé and toss your life into the wind by marrying the next guy to give a shit." I throw a sidelong glance at Darius. "No offense."

He nods. "None taken. I think we can all admit that we didn't make the best of decisions when we were young. I know Mae and I didn't take the traditional routes and that you're hurt Brandi, but you need to let that shit go. Mae and I don't have a lot, but we have love. And no matter what you may believe, we love this land. But we love our family more."

I sigh and look up at the setting sun. My broken heart may be old news to them, but it still feels fresh to me. But maybe they're right; I need to move on and maybe one day forgive Mae.

"Alright y'all, I may have overreacted a bit, but trust me, Byron Logan is the slimiest investor you could ever talk to, and that has nothing to do with our past. Give me some time to look at the balance sheets and see what options we have. Y'all know I do this for a living, right? I save farms. Why didn't you just come to me?"

Mae makes a sound of disgust. "Because you're a judgmental cow that needs to get some dick. Speaking of which, have you told that White boy from Africa that's had your nose wide-open for the better part of seventeen years that you're in love with him yet? Maybe if you had some business of your own, you'd leave us the fuck alone. Byron told me he was very interested in building his restaurant on Edenton Shores-he asked Byron to look into it for him."

Just when I felt something other than hatred for this chick....

I start toward her again, but Darius maneuvers her behind him before throwing her a lethal glare. He knows that was a low blow. I don't believe for one second Riddick asked Byron to get Edenton Shores for him. He'd never hurt me like that. *Would he?*

She also knows I hate when she refers to him as "That White boy." He's so much more. Riddick helped me pick up the pieces when she broke my heart. He didn't even know why, but he was there. Mae was my best friend until her betrayal. Even when we started having different interests, she was like a sister to me.

Mae sighs as she peeks around Darius. Her face is resigned. "Look Brandi, you tend not to listen to any voice but your own." She lifts her hands and turns to walk away. "But this time, you're going to have to come to a consensus... *with all of us.* You've got one month to figure out an alternative to us selling or we're moving forward." She throws me a look over her shoulder. "You know I have no problem fighting you in court. Fighting is what we do best."

Darius shrugs and throws me a conciliatory look before following her as she stomps away. I'm left standing alone in the middle of the field that tethers me to the earth when my life is an abyss of depression and destruction.

I can't lose Edenton Shores to Byron and his machinations, or I'll surely lose myself. I'll save it... to save me.

I need to talk to Riddick. He'll know what to do.

He always does.

Chapter 5

No Shame

Riddick

BRANDI NEEDS ME.

I got in my car as soon as she called.

I never should have stayed away from her. She left the farm crying and wouldn't give me any details on what went down at Edenton Shores today. But I can guess. I looked at the balance sheets Byron sent over before we met today. If I had checked my email last night and saw what his plans were, I could have saved myself some time and him an ass whooping.

No matter how pissed I am at Byron, the numbers don't lie. Edenton Shores is in trouble. There are two mortgages that are both behind. Foreclosure is only sixty days away. *What the hell have Mae and Darius been doing?* Why haven't they told Brandi anything? I wonder if Ciara knows. The farm is approximately $500,000 in debt. The only person I know with that kind of money is me; but Brandi nor Ellis would ever take my money. They'd rather die than take charity. I could try and secretly pay it off, but Brandi would never forgive me for that. She's too proud. So, this is truly a pickle.

My drive from Raleigh to Abbott Ridge reminds me why I stayed in North Carolina after college, instead of moving back home to South Africa.

I know better than anyone that Cape Town's beaches, wineries, and untouched game reserves are unrivaled in beauty, afforded pleasures, and adventure. But, east-central North Carolina's hilly Piedmont region and flat coastal plains make my heart ache with wonder.

Cape Town doesn't have majestic forests of hickory and oak trees that birthed this part of the state. The wilderness I regularly hike on weekends symbolizes an unbridled freedom missing from my home country. I love America, but I don't romanticize it.

I'll never forget that, like South Africa, freedom is not readily available to all in North Carolina. Apartheid's bloody shadow of racism is fresh. But America's Jim Crow and slavery eras of the past still pump blood into the systemic racism that stymies the American dream for many people of color. History has a sense of irony. At this moment in America, it seems like we might be ready to talk about it. Back home we had the Truth and Reconciliation Commission, but now it feels like it's impolite to even mention Apartheid.

My heart beats faster thinking about the woman who taught me how to see the world through this lens. Brandi never lets me forget my privilege, nor the bloody history of my new home. No matter how tidied up it seems.

Shit, even if America was only a bare wasteland left over from a zombie apocalypse, I'd still be here... *for her.* She snatches my breath away with just one look from her erotic black eyes. I crave her with a singular passion.

She just doesn't know it.

The beautiful creature has been my best friend for the past seventeen years. She's the one true constant in my life. My parents stay too busy with their game reserve and animal rights causes to pay me any real mind. It's been that way since I was a kid. I love them, and they took care of me, but I could never really talk to them. That's why I chose an American College.

I'm an only child, and I needed to make a life for myself some-where else. I had to find my tribe. Abbott Ridge was one of the few colleges that offered me a full scholarship to study chemistry, so I came. Little did I know that the real chemistry would happen the first day I met Brandi in passing. She was with her younger sister Ciara, and they were grabbing snacks from the vending machine. She didn't notice me, but I never forgot her. A few weeks later, I defended her in a dorm council meeting so that she could keep her cats for emotional support. I barely knew her but felt the primal need to protect her. I needed to see her happy.

Then a week later, Brandi and I met again on the quad. We ended up bonding over a bite of my Cinnabon- *that she was not ashamed to ask for-* and a subsequent conversation about the merits of Sir George Michael's voice and Jay-Z's wit on the Blueprint album. I found a like-minded audiophile that day.

Then I really fell for her.

I quickly tucked my initial feelings away. Within our first week of meeting all those years ago, she shared she was celibate and saving herself for an elusive soul mate that God prepared especially for her. The barrier she put up between us was perfectly constructed and immovable. No man has measured up. The ones that dared try to woo her bit the dust.

I needed her too much to allow that to happen to me. I kept my heart and mouth shut on the subject. I knew she was full of shit about her vow of celibacy, but I prided myself on avoiding futile endeavors.

Now that's all about change.

Brandi isn't waiting for an elusive divine match. *She's hiding from one.* She doesn't want any man's admiration, including mine, because she's scared. I don't know exactly what happened, but at least now I know it was Byron who broke her heart before we met during our freshman year. Just thinking about it makes me want to find the wanker again and tear him limb from limb for even hurting her. But, if she doesn't talk about it, neither will I. Byron blindsided me with the information, but I don't want her thinking she has to explain herself.

I remember the one and only time I challenged her vow of

celibacy and the circumstances leading up to it; she bit my head off and hid from me for an entire week. That was fourteen years ago at graduation. So, I let it go.

I figured that eventually her concrete dam of control would break and then I would help her swim in the emotional overflow when it did. Until then, I'd wait.

Plus, it's not like I've been pining away in misery. My six restaurants and wineries in Raleigh, Atlanta, and Miami keep me insanely busy. I've never had time to settle down. If I needed to blow off some steam, women were always willing and able. I let them know up front that my heart wasn't available, even as I let them have as much dick as they wanted.

I've broken some hearts over the years. Sadly, some women believed they could change my mind. They thought if they fucked me well enough, that I would discover I can't live without them. I hated when that happened, but there was and is only one woman on earth I can't live without. She is my best friend.

Hell, for the past year, I haven't even tried to have sex. I'm getting too old for the drama.

My dick only gets hard when I'm around or thinking of Brandi. It's been hell. I don't know when I needed more from her, but the change happened quickly. One thing's for sure, I can't go on like this. It's not healthy for either of us. Because even though she'll never admit it; I'm the constant in her life, too.

I didn't plan on coming to Homecoming this year, but now that I am, I'm making the trip worth my while. I'm not letting the weekend end without making Brandi mine. No matter what the costs, she will know how much I want and need her before I head back to Raleigh.

Shit, I also need to have sex before my dick explodes and apparently, he's decided that only Brandi will do.

I need to get started on the rest of my life. Something tells me when I have her, that's when my life will really begin. Success is empty without someone to share it with.

As I pull up to the Michael Jordan Gymnasium and Health

Center, I'm impressed. The new gymnasium is only a year-old and a far better gym than we had on campus when I was here. Its beautiful glass windows and spring domed roof looks celestial. The students and athletes have a world class facility to use. I donated a sizeable chunk of money for it to come to fruition. I see Abbott Ridge spent my five million dollars well.

Tonight, is the Alumni step show and the official kickoff to Homecoming Weekend. As an esteemed member of Psi Kappa Chi, I'd love nothing better than to pick up my old crimson and cream cane and show these Neos and young bucks how the old heads get down. But, I haven't practiced in a while and I won't disrespect my letters that way. I told Brandi I wouldn't be able to see her perform with her line sisters in celebration of the sorority's 100th year anniversary. Work was an easy excuse because I always work. I wasn't ready to deal with us yet.

But, after talking to her and hearing the anxiety in her voice, I couldn't stay away. I rearranged some meetings and canceled an event and now that I'm on campus; I feel alive again. It's been too long and I'm ready to see my kitten shake that beautiful jet-black mane of hers. I want to watch her ass shimmy in the sacred teal and orange of her sorority.

My phone rings and I look up to see one of the many women I've romanced in the past is calling me. Katrina Taylor is persistent. I know if I don't answer, the texts will follow next. She truly does not understand the meaning of the phrase casual fuck. I know Katrina's type. She's interested in my money. She ran through Raleigh's entire rotary club trying to marry rich. I silence my phone and focus on the one woman I know loves me for who I am. My heart thumps harder, knowing I'm only a few minutes from holding her in one of my infamous bear hugs.

I head backstage to get a glimpse of her before she goes on. If I see that she's Ok, my skin will stop burning with nervous energy. Backstage is hectic, with so many fraternities and sororities prepping for the show. The current members and alumni are rushing around making last-minute preparations. I push through the chaos to track her down. Probably should wait until after the show, but I'm too wired for that. I smile when I hear her voice.

"Ladies, we may be closer to forty than twenty, but our knees still got it. Don't let these Neos take all our shine tonight. We are going to show them how it's done!"

I chuckle, listening to Brandi give her sisters a pep talk. She could motivate a cow to run a country mile if she had the mind too. I stare at her while she gives instructions. She looks incredible. Her ebony skin shines while her hair swings shiny and thick down to her ass. She's in dark blue cut-off shorts that show off the bottom half of her sexy chocolate ass.

I groan, thinking about what it would feel like to take a bite out of that jiggling left cheek. *Because I will.* Her long legs support what looks like four or five inch fringed stiletto boots. I've seen the look before on Beyoncé when she re-enacted Homecoming as a tribute to Historically Black Colleges and Universities at Coachella. Abbott Ridge is not an official HBCU, but it has a thriving Black student population. Like Bey, Brandi's wearing an Orange Hoodie with the Greek letters of Rho Beta Chi in Teal Rhinestones across her chest. The hoodie is fitted and her full tits are pressed against the fabric.

Fuck! I want to drive into her until she forgets her damn name.

Before I can adjust the rock hard dick laying across my right thigh like a painful third arm, Brandi turns around and spots me. Her eyes catch mine and they dance. Brandi's surprised, but the joy on her face is undeniable.

She really missed me. She needs me.

Slowly, she takes in my body. Her eyes settle on my fitted Black jeans and the unmistakable bulge between my legs. Her eyes widen and her lips part slightly.

"Riddick," my name is a barely audible gasp.

She sees I'm hard for her, and she likes it. Or maybe it's just my imagination.

Either way, she's mine.

Chapter 6

No Way

Brandi

RIDDICK LOOKS *good enough to eat.*

I play it cool as I gaze at his chiseled chest and the tattoo peeking out from the unbuttoned top of his silk black shirt. I resist the urge to lick my lips as my eyes work their way down his torso.

What the fuck is that in his pants? *A baseball bat?* And why is he walking towards me with it? The better question is, why am I salivating?

Stop staring Brandi. Snap out of it.

He walks toward me, and I turn my head to tell myself that he's only my best friend. *Nothing More.* The mental pep talk does not snap me out of whatever trance I'm in.

When he's close enough, I take in his unique scent of money, musk, and man. My eyes snag on his dick again. I really should look up from his bulge, but I can't, because then I'll see him, and the way his eyes were burning a hole through me a second ago. I'll take my chances looking at the weapon he calls a dick.

This is ridiculous.

Finally, I tear my eyes away from him and look around. All my line sisters are dressed in outfits just as sexy as mine. That must be the reason he's so hard. They would arouse any man taking in this view. We may be 35 and over, but we all still got it. There's no denying that. The alumni step team stays in shape because we must. We train six months out from homecoming. We're in the best shape of our lives by the time we hit the stage for our grueling ten minute performance. So that hard-on is not for me. *It can't be.*

Riddick doesn't see me that way. He never has, I've made sure of it.

I look to my left and see Mandy Foster throw her long blonde hair over her shoulder and smile while stalking towards Riddick. I shake my head. She's always had a thing for him, and he's never given her the time of day. She should know by now that Barbie ain't his type. But I can't blame her for trying. He is sexy. If you're into that whole body of a God and face of Adonis thing.

Riddick Paul Kruger is Fine with a capital F! He's a solid 6'4, and is always only 180 pounds. He's relentless about maintaining that weight. I think keeping his playing weight makes him feel like he is still an athlete. He's a gym rat, but not obnoxiously. It's more motivating than unpleasant. Riddick pays attention to what he puts in his body and takes excellent care of himself. Something we all should do. He's invited me to the gym many times, but I've declined. I have a feeling his workouts are too intense for me. Plus, I'm pretty sure I'm not prepared to see him sweaty and shirtless.

Riddick's smooth skin is the color of an eggshell in the Fall and Winter months; and toasted almond milk in the Spring and Summer. He tans so easily that I often tease him about having some Blackness somewhere in his family tree. He always smiles and flashes me those two impossibly deep dimples as he says," Oh, I hope so."

Being a Black woman in a small southern town, there weren't many opportunities to become best friends with anyone that didn't look like me. There's no official line of segregation in Abbott Ridge, but unofficially everyone stays in their community and on their farms.

However, Abbott Ridge College has always been a place of coming together. When you step on campus, differences are celebrated. I was drawn to Riddick immediately, and I thought the fact that he was from South Africa was fascinating. After that meeting on the quad extolling the virtues of hip-hop and British pop music; I knew I wanted to talk to him every day for the rest of my life. But I also know if I let it go further than friendship; I'll lose him. I'm not enough to keep him. I couldn't even keep Byron Logan.

I've heard the legend that is Riddick Kruger. He's an amazing lover that fucked half the campus while we were in college. It never bothered me back then. I wanted to stay as far away from sex as possible, and he knew that. So, I never had to worry about him looking at me in that light. As we got older, he asked more questions about my choice of celibacy. I told him it was because of my faith. Truthfully, I've been paralyzed by one traumatic relationship for almost eighteen years now and I don't know how to get free.

But he might be the key, because the way he's looking into my soul right now is almost enough for me to throw fear into the wind.

"Well, if it isn't Riddick Kruger," I hear Mandy purr.

The grating sound of her voice knocks both Kruger and me out of our trance. She sidles up to Kruger and rubs her hands over his stomach while eying his dick. *She's so thirsty.* I want to get the poor girl a glass of water. She may be my line sister, but I swear if she doesn't get her hands off him, I'll cut her wiry ass.

"Long Time no see. Did you come to see me perform? You know I've still got all my moves."

I'm going to be sick. And Riddick looks like he's going to be as well. That's his fault. No one told him to use Mandy as his go-to fuck toy all throughout college. She's always thought she had claim to him, even though he never made the slightest gesture to claim her. Now, she's all over him like a cat with claws.

He clears his throat and seeks me out with his eyes. "Umm…

no, I'm actually here to support Brandi." He nods his head towards me, forcing Mandy to turn around. I give her a saccharine smile and wave. She rolls her eyes but recovers quickly.

"Oh yeah, I forgot she's like a little sister to you. Of course, you'd want to see her perform. But isn't it a bonus that you also get me out of the deal? Someone who knows how to use her body very well."

Bitch. Two can play this game.

I walk over to Kruger and step beside him. Placing my hand in his, I squeeze and throw him a quick wink before bringing his ring hand to my lips and brushing my lips over the back of his knuckles. *Sweet baby Jesus, his skin is incredible.* I feel his calluses on the inside of my hand, but the skin brushing my lips is soft as silk.

My poor neglected pussy is dripping from his sexy scent alone. I close my eyes and take a deep breath before I hear him clear his throat, soft enough for my ears. That's right, I had a reason to come over here, and getting high off the smell of his skin was not it. I glance at him and peep the right side of his mouth turned up in the beginning of a smile. I quickly look away and glare at Mandy.

"We are not siblings. Far from it, Mandy, what we are goes deeper than that. Wouldn't you agree, Riddick?"

My eyes never leave her scowl. Her eyes never leave my hand wrapped in his. She looks like she might combust, she's so angry.

Riddick turns to me and his jaw flinches. The look in his eyes is predatory and I get the distinct feeling that I finally opened a door he was seeking entrance into. "I definitely agree," his sexy voice grumbles. "We're the best part of each other."

His words almost knock me to my ass. *What the hell is that supposed to mean?* He returns my earlier gesture by flipping our clasped hands over and dropping kisses on the inside of my wrist. My knees buckle at the gesture and my breath catches. He chuckles and pulls me away from Mandy, winking as we turn to leave. "We'll see you around, Mandy. Break a leg."

When we get out of her view, I drop Riddick's hand and laugh. The sound is nervous and unnatural, but I follow through with it, anyway. Anything to break this awkward tension between us. But when I look up at Riddick's face, he doesn't look uncomfortable at all. He looks determined. I place my hand on my neck and swallow.

"Mandy is still hot for you. She never could keep her hands off you."

Riddick nods. "Yeah, she never could.' He steps closer to me, and I step back. Still, he stalks me until my back is against a wall and I realize we're practically alone on the side of the stage. He trails the back of his knuckles across my cheek and smirks.

"But you know, Kitten, I'm curious about your touch, not hers. Do you want me to touch you again?"

"Wh..wh..at." I stammer.

He nods. "Umm hmm. Unfortunately, Mandy has had the undeserved privilege of touching my body all over. I wasn't very discerning in the past. She's had her legs wrapped around my thighs, lips around my cock, her hands grabbing my ass as I thrust into her. But none of those touches set my entire body and soul on fire, like the brush of your lips against my hand a few moments ago."

Oh, God... his mouth. It's so dirty. Every word is going straight to my core.

Riddick steps into me, and I gulp at his closeness. Part of me is terrified of being pushed against a wall by such a powerful man. If he wanted to, he could trap me there with his weight. It reminds me of the first time Byron took my innocence. When I could not get away.

But the larger part of me is the calmest I've ever been. His scent and voice make me zone out into a happy place. I literally want to climb inside of him. Because he equals safety for me. My voice doesn't work, because I can't believe he's talking to me like this. Where did all this come from? He's never been so close. I've never felt the heat roll off him like this.

"Answer me." His voice is deep now. He's commanding me. It's a tone he's never used with me before, but fuck if I don't like it. "I don't enjoy asking questions that don't get answered, Brandi."

His lips graze over mine while he speaks. Jesus, I want his kiss so badly. All I would have to do is lean up and crush my mouth onto his. What harm would that do? Just one little kiss and then we can act like this craziness never happened. Can a kiss really change everything? Would it even mean anything to a man like Riddick?

It could also mean everything. He said I'm the best part of him. Maybe he wants this kiss as much as I do. *But we can't.* Because something tells me if I press my lips to his, it will be a moment defined by before and after. We will forever have to look at our friendship as before the kiss and after the kiss. And I'm not ready for that at all, because I'm not sure if I can physically give him anything beyond a kiss.

I look up and his eyes are penetrating my soul. He wants an answer and I have a feeling the only way I can get away without verbally giving him one is to kiss him. There's no way out and I'm lost in his gaze. Then I hear the start of Lil' Boosie's "Wipe Me Down" and I'm saved. That's the introduction to our set and I've got to get on stage.

I clear my throat and slide down and under his arm. "Umm, that's my cue. It's showtime."

He laughs, shakes his head, and pulls me closer to him before descending upon me with a tsunami of passion. His lips hit mine and the electricity between us zaps to life. The kiss is tender but demanding. There's no soft start. He licks the seam of my mouth to request entry, and once my lips part, it's a wrap. Kruger's tongue invades my mouth like he's searching for gold. He tastes like the cinnamon gum he chews since he stopped smoking ten years ago, and I swear it's an aphrodisiac. As soon as my mind registers the taste and smell, I kiss him back with equal fervor. My knees weaken as the seconds pass, and it's not until I moan like a wanton lover that he lets me go. That was not just a kiss, that was a declaration of sexual intent. *And I liked it.*

I'm fucked.

The music gets louder and in the distance, I hear my sisters calling my name with more urgency. I scurry away, watching Riddick wipe the side of his lips with his thumb and forefinger before finally turning round.

"Brandi." His voice booms, the command sending a pulse straight to my core. I pause.

"You will answer my question. Tonight. Enjoy your show,"

I stand there a second before I step into line and stroll on stage. My mind is trapped between Riddick's enormous arms, wondering how to tell him I love him, but that I can't ever cross the line from friendship to lovers with him.

I'm too broken.

Chapter 7

No Retreat

Riddick

I'M HARD AS STONE.

Kissing her may not have been the best idea.

Hell, watching Brandi perform isn't a good idea either.

Viewing her in that skimpy outfit backstage pushed me to mark her mouth in the most delicious way. Now that she's stepping and dancing in those damn shorts, all I want to do is jump on stage and haul her ass over my shoulder caveman style.

I'll face the consequences later.

It doesn't help that she's eye-fucking me from the stage with an angry and aroused stare. I threw her off her game backstage, but I don't care. Brandelyn Armstrong hates losing control of anything, but I know that's exactly what she needs to do. I want her without control and trembling beneath me; writhing from the pleasure my hands, dick, and tongue deliver.

She should be worshiped and willed into submission. *It's time.*

I don't know what took me so long to figure it out. It's always been her since the day we met. She fascinates me. Her very essence makes me feel hard. I can't remember the last time I was around her that my dick wasn't at least standing at half-mast. I've simply learned to live with a chronic case of blue balls when I'm around her, because I won't touch her. She resolved that wasn't what she wanted from any man. I respect that. Even now, with my mind made up; she will have to beg me to fuck her before I act. I need her complete submission and unequivocal consent because I'll die before I harm her.

She's mad that I limited our contact this year, but I couldn't torture myself anymore. It was physically and emotionally painful to be around her.

The first three months she didn't even notice I'd withdrawn, or if she did, she never said a word about it. The indifference angered me, so I tried to fuck through my hurt pride. When I couldn't even get hard for another woman; I really got pissed.

I spent the next three months trying to figure out how to keep her in my life without her being the object of my affection. At least I was less hostile. I took her calls to keep tabs on her safety and well-being but kept the conversations brief. I made up every excuse in the book to not visit her or Abbott Ridge, no matter how much she hinted and asked. It was easier said than done, because there's always something going on in town that we usually attend together.

In the Spring it's the Spring Fling; a street festival with food vendors. Typically, I drive one of my food trucks up for the event so Brandi and I can work the hungry crowd together. She's always a trooper, doing any menial task needed to make my truck a success. It never felt like working with her by my side.

In the Fall we hook-up for the Harvest Moon Festival and Homecoming. During the holidays, we count down until it's time to drink hot chocolate and look at all the Christmas lights around town during Abbott Ridge Lights Up. I looked forward to those scheduled events with her, so by the time we missed the Harvest Moon Festival last month, I decided enough was enough. It was time to man up and make Brandi mine. I just didn't know how.

I couldn't get my shit together, so I told her my new restaurant Busu was having a big event, and that I wasn't coming to Homecoming. It shocked her to see me tonight. Even though she called me crying a few hours ago, I'm sure she thought I'd have to wait until the weekend was over to address it.

Good. I needed to surprise her to get her genuine response.

Brandi is used to me, and her reactions are rehearsed. I'm tired of the artificial distance when there is obviously so much chemistry. She likes to be around me because I provide her security and I've never pushed her out of her comfort zone. But that's no longer enough for me and I know it's not enough for her either.

"We Are Rho Beta Chi... Fierce and Fine...." Brandi and her sisters repeat the same chant they do at every performance, but instead of looking out into the audience, Brandi's eyes lock on to mine. She looks like she's trying to solve a puzzle, and I throw her a smug smile. I know I was a bastard for kissing her like I did and sending her on stage shaken up, but it had to be done. I won't allow her to hide from the possibility of us anymore.

When the ladies clear the stage, I rush to meet them and find Brandi with her back against a wall and her breathing labored. Her hands are on her knees and she's trying to catch her breath. No one else seems to notice she looks like she's about to pass out.

Did she eat enough today? She might be dehydrated.

Where the hell is Ciara?

Pushing people out of the way, I rush over and crouch down until we're at eye level. Rubbing firm circles across her back, I used my other hand to lift her chin so that her eyes settle on me.

"Brandi... What's wrong? Breathe baby, just breathe."

She keeps her eyes steady on mine and I wipe the sweat from her brow. When her breathing slows, she drops her head on my shoulder.

"I'm OK. I guess I'm out of shape. That routine took a bit out of me."

I look at her skeptically. "You sure that's all it is? Could it possibly be that you didn't eat enough today?"

Her eyes burn right through me. I know her eating habits are a touchy subject, but I don't give a fuck. I need to know she's taking care of herself. She is so obsessive about what she puts in her body that it becomes dangerous, and I have to step in. It's happened before.

"Riddick, I'm fine. Give me your water."

I hand her my bottle of water and she takes a long swig. While she drinks, I look her over and assess the color of her beautiful face and her bright almond-shaped eyes. "Hmmm, you look pale. Tell me what you ate today," I say more sharply than I intend.

Brandi rolls her eyes at my tone, but at least it gets her going. She stands straight up, but a bit too fast. She places her hand on her forehead, trying to steady herself. I scowl and snatch her hand away.

"Are you dizzy? Do we need to go to urgent care?" I'm about to drag her there until she stops me.

"Riddick. No! OK, maybe I only had time for a cup of coffee and a side salad today. But that's because that fight with Mae threw my timing off and took a lot of energy. I promise you; I meant to go home and fix myself something to eat, but I ran out of time."

I raise an eyebrow. I knew she probably had words with Mae, but it sounds like a bit more went down.

"Fight? What fight? Did you go over there and start some shit Brandi after I distinctly told you not to? I swear I will tan your hide if you were brawling."

She rolls her eyes. "Oh, hush Riddick! You're not the boss of me," she hisses. "You shouldn't have told me about her shenanigans if you didn't want me to put my foot up her ass. But don't worry dad, we hugged it out before I left. Her idiot husband ensured it."

She's being a brat, but I nod. Thank God Darius is good for something.

I look down at her hands and see that she finished my entire bottle of water. Maybe she was just thirsty, or…. *Could it be?*

I cup the right side of her jaw and look into her eyes. With my left hand, I push her long hair behind her shoulders and trace her eyebrow with one finger. I move closer and her breath hitches until she closes her eyes tight at my touch.

"Easy," I mumble and smile. "Do you think you might have had a mild panic attack from the kiss I gave you before the show?"

Her eyes fly open, and she lifts her chin before throwing her shoulders back. She looks like a sexy soldier prepared for battle. "Riddick. It was just a kiss... and it was silly and uncalled for. Why did you do that, anyway?"

Silly... Did she just call my kiss silly?

Silently, I count to five and move close enough for my lips to skim her ear as I lean in and whisper. "No, Brandi. That was to get your attention, and it worked because ever since that moment, you have been focused right here." I step back and point two fingers to my eyes. "That kiss rocked your world, and that's why you're backstage trying to catch your fucking breath."

I hear her whimper before her nostrils flare, "Whatever, Riddick. Don't flatter yourself." Her attempt at a push feels more like a warm embrace. I smirk while she continues her rant. "You caught me off guard, that's all. You're lucky I didn't take your balls out to lunch with my knee!"

I chuckle. "Yes, I guess I am. That would have hurt." I reach out and take a strand of her hair in my hand and twirl it. "So, fucking beautiful..." I mumble.

Her eyes widen. "Wh-Wh-What did you say?"

"I think you heard me just fine. I said you're beautiful."

I take another look at her face, and she's still flushed. Despite my display a moment ago, I'm not a complete asshole. I know her current state is not just from my kiss. She needs to eat.

"You don't look too good, Brandi. I think your blood sugar is low again. I swear, if you don't start eating more, I'm going to create a food plan for you to follow and I won't tolerate any deviance from it. You've got to take better care of yourself." I stroke another strand of hair out of her face. "Now, where's a bathroom you can use to freshen up? You killed it out there tonight, and I'm taking you to the Waffle House to celebrate."

Her entire face lights up. I knew that would make her happy-*extra calories be damned.* We used to always go to Waffle House to end the first night of homecoming weekend. Usually, we would be drunk and in desperate need of some greasy food and water.

"OK," she practically sings. "The bathroom is right around the corner. I'll be right back."

She turns to pull away, but I keep a hold of her elbow. "I'll go with you. I need to make sure you don't have another dizzy spell."

Brandi sighs but doesn't fight me. We continue down a dark hallway and come to a door that looks like the entrance to a broom closet. Immediately, I think of how dangerous it is back here. You can't be seen or heard this far back from the stage area. I'm glad I walked back here with her.

When she reaches the door, she releases my hand and walks in, closing the door behind her. It's silly, but I already miss her touch. Just when I talk myself out of going in behind her to kiss her; I hear her curse and the door swings open.

"What is it?" I ask.

"The lightbulb is dead, and I can't see shit."

I look behind her and see that it's a single bathroom, only the size of a closet. I turn on my phone, open the flashlight app, and follow her in. With the light shining, she can see her way to the sink. She looks at me with a bit of shock, but I only shrug.

She murmurs thanks and turns to splash some water on her face. She pulls a wet wipe from a little basket on the tiny sink counter and wipes all the make-up off her face.

Good, she's too pretty for that nonsense, anyway.

While she works, my eyes drink her in. She's slightly bent over the sink to look in the mirror and I can't take my eyes off the bits of ass hanging from her shorts. I want to bite her there hard and then use my tongue to smooth away the sting. See, this is the problem. I'm a nasty fuck, and I'm not sure if Brandi will be down. I don't want to scare her off.

My cock swells, and I discreetly adjust myself with my free hand. I'm so caught up in the fantasy of what I want to do to her ass that I don't hear Brandi calling my name.

"Riddick! What the hell are you thinking about? And why are you staring at my ass like a creeper?"

I didn't think she would call me on it. But then again, that's exactly what Brandi does. I've seen her dress men down for less on the street. Since I've never allowed myself to get caught openly staring before; I wasn't prepared for the rebuke. And now, I'm pissed. Did she just call me a creeper? Like I'm just some random dude salivating over a perfect ass that defies gravity?

Hell, if she already thinks I'm one, I may as well creep over and see how she reacts with a bit more of me in her space.

Chapter 8

No Air

Riddick

So, I creep…

Walking closer and keep my eyes on hers. Silently, I ask permission to demand her submission. I have no doubt that her increased breaths are in response to the look of hunger on my face. I damn near smell her excitement. Once I'm close enough to touch her, I stroke her cheek with my finger, and she leans into my touch. She's not overwhelmed. She's aroused.

I tilt my head to study her. Can I do this? Will our friendship survive the onslaught?

Fuck it, I'm shooting my shot.

"Brandi, I have no intention of making you uncomfortable. But as I'm sure you know; your ass is a work of art; so why wouldn't I stare? Why wouldn't I admire one of God's finest creations? I'm a man and you, my sweet Kitten, are very much a woman."

Her voice wobbles. "But you're… you're Riddick. You don't care about my ass."

She says the last words with such conviction that I laugh. I've done Brandi no favors by acting like I'm immune to her beauty. Women talk, so she's aware of my sexual reputation and the pleasure I bring the fairer sex. Hell, she even told me a time or two that I'm little more than a man-whore. But when it comes to her, she thinks I'm some sort of asexual playmate. Nothing is further from the truth.

I rub up and down her arms before kissing the side of her head. "Sweetheart. I promise you I care very much about that sweet ass of yours. You didn't listen. I told you on New Year's Eve that the next time I saw you, I would kiss you and make you mine, and I meant it. I'm over just being your friend, Brandi." She's quiet, so I take her hand and squeeze tight. "I want to be your lover, friend, and everything in between."

Brandi stares at me for a moment in shock. I wait a few moments and she finally speaks.

"You want to be my everything? Why?"

I don't dignify her foolish question with a verbal response. *I want her because she's perfect.* Instead, I drop my phone down on the floor and cloak us in darkness. With both hands now free, I place one on either side of her head and bring her lips to mine for a kiss. Gently, I massage my fingers into her scalp as I lick her lips, beckoning her to open for me. Once she obliges, I dive deep inside her warm mouth and give my kitten a crash course on what it means to be devoured. My tongue tangos with hers, but she never gets to take the lead. I tilt her head to my liking and kiss her harder and longer until she's breathless.

When I pull back to check on her; I'm prepared to be cursed out. *There's a 50/50 chance I may get slapped.* Instead, she makes a small noise that sounds like... *well, damn...* it sounds like a purr. Then she grabs me by my shirt to pull me back down on her lips. This time, I revel in her power. I let her explore the kiss on her own terms for a while and relish once again in her taste.

During it all, my cock grows to his full length. *There's no way she doesn't feel that.* I press my luck and grab her ass, pushing her against my length, and instead of a reprimand, I'm awarded with a moan.

A. Fucking. Moan...She's trying to kill me.

I pull away from the kiss and watch the dazed look in Brandi's eyes. In the dark, I can't see her too well, but her eyes outshine any darkness. "Do you feel that, Brandi? Can you feel how hard I am for you? Do you feel what you do to my cock? That's why I stare at your ass, Kitten. You drive me fucking crazy."

I drop my hand down and gently pet her sex. My touch extracts a groan as I stroke her dampness through the denim. I can't believe how soaked she is. *Or that I'm touching her.*

"Fuck! Brandi, your pussy is pouring. Is the honey trapped in these sexy ass shorts for me? Are you going to let me make your pretty pussy purr? Can I taste the desire you have for me?"

She nods and harshly whispers, "Yes, please." She's desperate to come. Before she changes her mind, I swiftly unbuckle and drag the denim shorts down her ass and shapely thighs, pausing on my way back up to take a bite of her right thigh.

"You don't need these," I mumble as I snap her lace thong in two places. Then I let it fall to the ground. "Turn around and open your legs a little wider for me, baby. Place your hands on the sink. I'm going to fuck you with my fingers until you're gushing down my hand. Would you like that?"

Brandi nods, and I stop petting her.

"No Kitten, I want your words. Would you like that?"

"Yes, Riddick. Please fuck me."

I smirk. *Today my fingers, tomorrow my dick.*

I crack the door to the bathroom slightly to allow some light to shine on the mirror above the sink. There's no way I'm missing her facial features the first time I make her come. Plus, I want her to see herself come undone. She will witness her body unravel at my hands.

Brandi shoots a quick glance at the cracked door but doesn't protest. I swear, she pushes her ass back up against me harder; nudging me to get going. *Why the little exhibitionist!* She likes the idea that we could get caught. Too bad, I'd never let that happen. Now that I'm holding her, this ass is only for me.

I get down on my hunches behind her and bite her ass cheeks before slapping them both. The firm smacks cause her dimpled ass to jiggle and fuck me if I don't want to bust a nut right there. I alternate and give her another six or seven smacks, her moans telling me I'm on the right track. I stand up behind her and waste no time thrusting two fingers into her wet center.

"Fuuuuuuck, Riddick." She moans.

I chuckle and growl into her ear. "You hear your pussy, kitten? It's so wet from that little spanking I gave you. I want to get down on this floor and have you sit that wet motherfucker on my face so I can eat you until you see stars."

"Oh, God…" she moans and closes her eyes. I slap her ass.

"No Kitten, eyes open. Look how beautiful you are with my fingers in your pussy."

The warmth in her eyes returns to mine in the mirror and I damn near melt.

"Yes, Brandi. That's what I want to do, but we don't have time tonight." *And I'm too fucking tall to lay on this floor.* "But that doesn't mean you won't come. Oh baby, you're going to come so hard…"

I lift her sweatshirt and pull her bra down. Using my free hand, I test the weight of each breast before twisting and pinching her nipples. Her moan is a mix of pain and pleasure. I add a third finger to her soaking core and push in and out of her with a pounding rhythm. When I feel her walls quiver, I know she's going to blow at any moment.

Reaching over, I inhale her peach scent and bite down on the side of her neck while I curl my fingers to touch the rough G spot at the front of her walls. Watching the mirror, I see her orgasm before I hear it. Her mouth forms a perfect O and her eyes lock onto mine. I turn her head to take her scream in my mouth while I continue to rocket my fingers in and out of her. She rides one orgasm and then two more before she finally falls off the top of the rollercoaster I've pushed her down. Never leaving her hooded eyes, I lick my fingers clean and moan in appreciation of her delicious flavor.

Turning her around, I lace soft kisses all over her chin, lips, and wet cheeks.

My kitten is crying.

She collapses into my arms, and I know that she needs reassurance more than anything. She needs to know that I will always be her friend, even when I'm her lover. I'll do anything to make this woman happy. Whatever it takes to save Edenton Farms, I'm going to do it. Even if what it takes makes her angry in the short-term.

Holding her head to my chest, I kiss the top of her head and murmur how good and sweet she is. How perfect she was.

She stays quiet. *Too quiet,* while I roll her shorts back over her hips. Silently, she pulls up her bra and pushes her sweatshirt down. I look into her eyes, willing her to say something... anything. But it takes a while for her to come all the way down.

Finally, she smiles and releases a shaky breath. "I'm starving."

God, I love her.

"Ok, Kitten," I smile. "Let's go. I'll buy you two pecan waffles. It's my treat."

She smirks. "It better be."

Brat...

Saturday: The Tailgate

Love, like rain, does not choose the grass on which it falls.
-South African Proverb

Chapter 9

No Calls

Brandi

LAST NIGHT WAS A CLUSTERFUCK.

I should be mad as a wet hen. Riddick turned my perfectly fine world upside down. The past seventeen years, he's been my rock and best friend. *A very platonic best friend.* Now he may be something in between.

I really thought he was joking when he told me last New Year's Eve; the next time he saw me, he would kiss me and make me his. Now I'm wondering if that's the real reason he hasn't come to Abbott Ridge this year. Maybe he wasn't ready to make good on his promise. I wonder what made him brave enough last night.

After the earth-shattering orgasm he gave me, all I wanted to do was curl up in his lap and suck my damn thumb until I fell asleep. I have never experienced an orgasm like that in my life. I didn't know my body could explode with such pleasure. My vibrator doesn't begin to compare to the way his strong fingers felt inside me.

Is that what I miss when I turn down date after date? *I doubt it.* I think Riddick is a different breed of man altogether.

He played my body like an instrument he mastered years ago. I felt like I was utterly his while wrapped in his arms. It's silly because no one ever belongs to Riddick. He doesn't have girl-friends. He never keeps a woman longer than a month. Riddick meets them, charms them, fucks them, and then dumps them. I never really cared before, and to be honest, I shouldn't care now. It's not like we had sex. Yet, him touching me the way he did feels more intimate. His attention was deliberate. Ooh, I shudder just thinking about it.

Riddick would never ghost me. We're too close for that. And I also know he would never consciously hurt me. However, I need to save him from himself. What happened last night can never happen again. If it does, it will end in disaster. He's not cut out to be the man I need him to be and I'm sure as hell not the woman he wants long-term.

I step out of my comfortable White down-covered bed and stretch. My cats Tristan and Isolde scurry around my ankles and I smile. I reach down to rub behind their ears before standing to check their bowls of food in the kitchen. When I reach the bay window where they both like to lounge and soak in the sun, I look down and notice empty water bowls. I feel a pang of guilt. I was so discombobulated last night that I forgot to refill their water bowls.

"Oh, you're thirsty huh? Give mama a second." I purr. They throw me looks of extreme judgment. Tristan even sends me a sassy meow. You think they'd cut me some slack; I never forget to fill their bowls when I come home.

Everyone jokes I treat my cats better than people. In some ways, that's true. Neglecting them last night was truly a one off. It isn't my fault my best friend surprised me with a mind-blowing orgasm when I least expected it. Me being so distracted that I forgot to fill their water bowls last night is further proof that romance and relationships are nothing but trouble.

Peace is my home. I bought this place four years ago after my grandmother died, and it's been my haven. It's a 200-year-old mansion sitting on 40 acres of farmland. It was a plantation once, but now it's my home. I board my horses and grow the same grapes my grandmother did to make her homemade wine. The house itself is an ode to modern farmhouse chic. I have enough shiplap, crisp white walls, fresh greenery, and sparkling chandeliers to make Joanna Gaines gasp.

Once I fill their bowls, and both my babies are happily licking their thirst away, I put on a brave face and check my phone while I brew myself a latte. My Nespresso Creatista Pro by Breville is hands down the favorite thing in my house. I don't play with my coffee.

While I wait for my drink to brew, I face the music. *Riddick's ringtone.*

Truthfully, I heard his missed calls last night after he dropped me off and made it home. I just couldn't bring myself to answer.

The ride to Waffle House was quiet and comforting. But once we got inside, and I filled my belly, Riddick laid his heart on the table. His words haunting me the rest of the night.

I want us to be together... romantically. It's time to take this friendship to the next level. Time to confirm what everyone else already knows. You belong to me, and I belong to you. Brandi, I want to be everything for you. Will you let me?

I had no answer for him, but he was OK with that. Everything that happened was still too raw. After we left the Waffle House, I needed to sort out my feelings on the matter and prepare a response. I couldn't talk to him with only my emotions to guide me.

Nope, this lawyer needs logic.

There were two missed calls from Riddick last night. He's probably pissed I didn't let him know I got to bed OK. He's protective. In his mind, anything can happen between me walking into my home and laying down for the night. I also have two missed calls from my grandfather this morning, but after fighting Mae, I'm not ready to hear him cuss me out.

There's also one surprising text from Riddick. He hates texting. He complains it's nothing more than a brief email. And he hates that even more. I pour my latte, take a seat at my kitchen island, and eagerly open the message. After the first sip, I wince at the temperature and Riddick's soft command.

Riddick: *We're talking about us today. Get your mind right. I'll see you at the tailgate. Meet me at the Psi Kappa Chi tent.*

Shit. What about us?

How do I feel about last night and his demand I become his? I'd love to pretend that I'm confused by his behavior. But I'm not. Riddick always goes for what he wants with full gusto. Knowing how he operates; he's been planning that full court press for a while. *But why?*

If I'm honest, his touch didn't befuddle or shock me as much as it settled me. The moment his lips touched mine, everything in my tightly controlled world unwound. In the wind down came a freedom and peace that I've never felt. A peace Riddick was certain that I needed. That was clear by his actions. Riddick Kruger does nothing he's uncertain about.

But that doesn't make this all OK.

He's confusing the hell out of me.

First, he tells me he's not even coming into town, but he shows up and manhandles me like I'm his. *The unmitigated gall!*

To be fair, I called him upset and crying; I should have known he wouldn't let that go unanswered. Then I started flirting with him when I saw Mandy trying to put her hands all over him. That shit was uncalled for. I may have pushed it far with the kiss to his knuckles, but he knows I don't like her. He should not have taken that as an invitation to do something devilish.

Riddick warned me what would happen the next time he saw me, and last night was the next time. Maybe I was waiting for him to fulfill his promise. *But I'm not ready to admit that.* I don't know what to do about it all. And what a thing to figure out. I spent the last half of my life making sure things like this didn't happen to me.

If Riddick knew the details of how Byron lied and broke my heart, he would never have crossed that line. Hell, he doesn't even know I was engaged to Byron. I'm sure he thinks I'm just his overly cautious and controlled kitten. But there's more to my motives.

I don't know how to get over the hurt that Byron caused. So instead of trying to get over it, I've lived through it by keeping my heart and body locked away.

Then here Riddick comes kicking down the door, waving a 44, and all I can scream is Riddick, don't kiss me no more. I stare at my latte and laugh at myself for misquoting The Notorious B.I.G.'s lyrics and get ready for the day. Biggie's problematic line from the song *Get Money* is exactly how I felt last night. Riddick waged war on my emotions, even if it was in the most pleasant and delicious way.

What to do? I can't lose him as a friend, but I can't handle him as a lover.

I'll dwell on this later because today is the Abbott Ridge homecoming game and tailgate. I plan to pick up Ciara, roam from tent to tent, and be drunk by 3:00 pm. Reliving my college days with Ciara takes precedence over all of this. *Sisters over misters.* Nothing comes before her, coffee, or wine. So, instead of responding to Riddick's text, I turn my phone off and step into the shower.

Once I step in, I let the hot water run over me and my skin tingles just thinking about those lips being where his fingers were last night. The filthy promise he whispered in my ear kept me up half the night. *Lord, keep my mind sweet Jesus.*

Riddick is sexy as hell. He always has been. I know if I ever see him naked again, I'll probably come in my panties on sight. I saw him in all his naked glory once five years ago by accident when I was staying with him in Miami during the opening of his restaurant, *Beso*, at Cocoa beach. His oceanfront villa is huge, and I got lost looking for the bathroom. Riddick has this thing against en suites. He adamantly believes that your bathroom should be separate from your bedroom. I can hear his voice now.

I don't want to poop anywhere near where I sleep.

So, he has a lot of bathrooms, but they're all in the hallways. I went into the wrong one while he was coming out of the shower and his body assaulted my senses with miles of sexy skin covered in delicious tattoos, rippling muscles, and a pair of strong thighs. Not to mention a dick that rivals the size of the cane he carries when stepping with his fraternity.

That thing needs its own license.

At the time we laughed about it. We knew everything else about each other, so it wasn't a big deal seeing one another naked. At least that's the way Riddick posited it. For me, it became fodder for plenty of sexy dreams for the next couple of years. I touched myself over and over, thinking about that day.

Now that I've felt his lips, this deluxe shower head is about to do my throbbing pussy a real service. I've got to take the edge off. If I don't, there's no way I'll make it through tailgating without letting Riddick bend me over a picnic table or cooler to have his way with me again.

Closing my eyes, I lean my head against the tile to think about his sexy baritone voice and how he sounds when he calls me kitten. I imagine the fall of his lips grazing my ear as he talked to me last night, telling me all the possessive things he will do. How he will make me his. When I remember the way, he rumbled the word mine against my lips. I let go. The extra jet in my shower head coupled with the memory is enough to make me moan out loud and call his name. I let my release run with the water and I moan as I come strong, imagining it's his lips on my slick pussy and not a 1,000-dollar shower head.

Damn, this is a mess.

Chapter 10

No Choice

Riddick

MAYBE THAT'S Brandi finally calling me back...

"Boy, have you seen my hard-headed granddaughter? I can't get up with her this morning and I need to know what's going on in that stubborn head of hers. What in the world would make her fight Mae? Her own flesh and blood! She knows I wouldn't agree to sell this land if it wasn't necessary. No need to fistfight over it."

It's 7:00 am and the last voice I expect to hear over the phone is the deep, demanding baritone of Ellis Armstrong III. No one else has the balls to call me boy. If his surly ass is calling me; shit must be serious. I want to ask him how he, the kettle, can call the pot, his granddaughter, black. They're both stubborn as two mules. But I won't. Ellis would hand me my proverbial hide.

Plus, I no longer view Brandi as simply stubborn. She definitely can be-ignoring my calls last night is a perfect example of that. But she's also passionate, unmovable, and steadfast. Once Brandi finds a cause, whether it be a person or the piece of land that her family farmed on for the past 150 years, she will not let it go without a fight.

Her grandfather Ellis shares the same level of passion for both Brandi and Edenton Shores. He loves that girl more than anything in this world. Well, almost anything. Because once Ellis

Armstrong makes his mind up about something, it's a wrap. If he's calling Brandi hardheaded and stubborn about this land fight. Then he's ready to sell. Brandi will be heartbroken, and that doesn't sit well with me at all.

I clear my throat and sit-up in bed. If I'm going to carry on a conversation with the formidable Ellis Armstrong; I need to have my wits about me.

In person, he's a force. Ellis Armstrong III stands at 6'8 and 280 pounds. I doubt the man has ever picked up an actual fitness weight, but he's solid muscle. Muscle forged from the hard work and heartache inherent to any man his age that was born and raised on a farm. He's the color of tobacco smoke and his coal-black eyes drill into you until you give up every secret you own. I'm glad we're speaking over the phone, or I'd surely end up telling him more than he needs to know about me and his favorite granddaughter.

I yawn and wipe a hand over my face. "Good morning to you, too. Mr. Ellis."

He grumbles like the local black bears he's always bragging about beating in his youth.

"Boy, don't sass me. I know what time it is, and it was a good morning two hours ago, when the good Lord had his cock to crow. It's damn near noon now."

No, it's not.

I ignore his reprimand but give him the information he needs. The faster he gets it, the faster I can carry my ass back to sleep.

"Sir, Brandi is not answering my calls, so I don't know where she is."

My answer is a bit of an exaggeration, but it should throw him off her scent and off my phone. Truth is, Brandi's probably at home drinking a latte from the beautiful expresso machine I bought her two years ago for Christmas, but that's neither here nor there.

I hear him spit his tobacco into a can before he lays into me. It's a nasty habit that most tobacco farmers around here have.

Brandi has tried everything to make him stop. But he's ninety and healthy, so it's far too late for that.

"Boy, what do you mean she ain't answering your calls? You are the only person Brandi talks to when she's in one of her anger spells. If she's mad at you, then we're all going to hell in a handbasket."

I chuckle. Mostly because he's right. I'm usually the one that calms Brandi down when she's worked up. "Mr. Ellis, I know, but I think I did something unpardonable. Well, at least your granddaughter thinks so. Point is, she won't pick up the phone."

He grunts. "What did you do to mess with my baby girl? Do I need to get ole Jeanie and ride by your house for a chat?"

Knowing that Ole Jeanie is his favorite shotgun, I quickly disabuse him of that notion. "Oh no sir, you know Brandi is a queen and I treat her like one. I just may have told her it's time she became more than just my friend over waffles last night. That declaration sent your granddaughter running."

I'm leaving out vital information, but he doesn't need to know about the bathroom escapade.

He laughs. A rare feat for Ellis Armstrong. The man is serious as a heart attack 99.9% of the time. "Oh shucks, that's all? You can fix that, boy. As a matter of fact, I'm telling you to fix it. And quick. We don't have time for you to dilly dally about my granddaughter at a time like this. We all know she loves you."

A smile breaks across my face. I'm glad they all know what I'm not so sure of. But I still refrain from telling him I popped up on his granddaughter and kissed her senseless. I wouldn't dare tell him I told her she was going to be mine in every way a woman can belong to one man. You can't tell a woman like Brandi Armstrong she belongs to you without counting the cost of such an endeavor. I know nothing about this will be easy. Her grandfather is in denial, but I'll play along.

"Easy you say? Well, let's hope so. I told her we need to talk about everything before the sun sets today, so I'm confident I'll see her this afternoon during the tailgate. Is there anything I can help you with in the meantime? Is there a message you want me to relay?"

Ellis spits and snorts. "What makes you so sure she is going to show up where you might be, if she's as mad as you say she is? I said it would be easy to fix, not quick. My granddaughter is just like me. She's awful good at holding a silent grudge."

I swing my legs over the side of the bed and stand to face my day. I think about his last words and smirk. The moment my lips landed on Brandi; I melted any future grudge. I felt the way her body quivered beneath mine when she came undone in my arms. Her knees were jelly. When I slipped my hand between the tight denim fabric of her daisy dukes and thrust into her bare pussy, I found her soaking wet. She's mad, but she's also overwhelmed and curious. Her body wants to know what it will feel like to be loved by more than just my hands. Her mind just hasn't caught up yet. That's because she does not know how good it can be between us inside and outside of the bedroom. I aim to show her.

"Let's just say I got it on good authority that she's going to show."

Because I told Ciara to bring her straight to my tent at the tailgate.

Ellis takes a deep breath, but I hear his wariness over the phone. He loves his three granddaughters more than anything in the world. He and Ma Kate, his wife of 55 years before she went home to be with the Lord a few years ago, practically raised all three of them after their parents died in a tragic boating accident. Brandi and Mae were thirteen and fourteen, respectively.

Brandi never talks about it, but I know she thinks about it. Now Ellis has two of the most precious people to him on earth at odds with each other. On one hand, he's got Brandi, who wants to hold the farm in Memorial forever. Whether it's a profitable farm does not factor into her calculations. She's made Ellis mighty proud over the years and he dotes on her. I thought his grin would split his face wide open when Brandi graduated from law school.

Then he has Mae. By Brandi and the world's measure, she was

a disappointment. She dropped out of high school and married Darius, hoping he'd make it to the league. He didn't, and they both stayed on the land to work it by necessity. They also took care of Ellis when Ma Kate died. He wasn't fit to do anything but lie in his bed and die of a broken heart. Brandi helped to nurse Ma Kate at the end of her life when she was battling cancer, and that took everything extra out of her. She didn't have the room to deal with the farm or Ellis' grief in the aftermath. But Mae did. And no matter what the reason was, she and Darius have worked the land and helped Ellis manage the farm for the past few years. I know Brandi hates to admit it, but they know more about the finances and state of Edenton Shores than she does.

"Son, there's no way around it. Edenton Shores is losing money left and right. Small tobacco and cotton farms can't make the money they used to. The corporate farms produce way more for cheaper. The way I see it, if we lease half of our land and sell the rest to this Byron fellow, not only would Mae, Ciara and Brandi be set for life. So would my great-grand Toya.

I'm an old man and I won't live forever. I've got to make sure my girls are taken care of. Darius is nice enough, but that boy ain't got the good sense that God gave a sloth. Mae has a good heart, but money motivates her too much. She won't make sound decisions that will benefit everyone. Ciara doesn't give a horse's ass. While Brandi is too smart for her own good and will only alienate everyone with her plans to keep the land at all costs.

She fights for all the Black farmers' rights around here, so she automatically thinks a corporate farm is bad and it's just a way of taking our land. But I don't care about this land if my folks can't eat. She doesn't know how to prioritize what really matters. You've got a head for business; you know we can't keep this farm as it is. She needs to see that. I thought you might help her through it, but you're too slow or too scared to really make Brandi yours. I can't trust she'll be in good hands if you can't even convince her to hold yours."

Damn. That last line of his rant was a low blow. But I've got to admit he has a point. I'm not currently in a place to be able to truly influence Brandi's decision about the farm. That's going to take time, and Mr. Ellis wants me to run in like a bull. But with Brandi, I've got to come in like a stealth panther. The moment she feels the wind shift, she will take off running. This is a war of inches, not miles. But perhaps, I can help in other ways.

"I read the balance sheet Byron had, but how much are you really in the red, Mr. Ellis?"

"Boy, I can't even tell you. We are about two crops behind. That Covid-19 mess sure ain't helping either. I lost a lot of good and dependable workers. If we don't get a big money dump soon, we're going to lose it all anyway, and that's what I think Brandi does not understand. She needs to help look over the contract and work with Mr. Byron to get us the best deal. I know he broke their engagement all those years ago and got caught up in a mess with Mae. But ain't he a friend of yours? You think he'd really fleece us?"

A mess with Mae? Interesting...

"Yes, I think he would." I answer quickly as I walk into my walk-n closet and pull out a pair of dark jeans and a soft, white V-neck T-shirt. I swear, Armani cotton feels like silk on the skin. *I need a casual cool look for today.*

Byron has no heart. He's always been loyal to me, but cut-throat and shrewd in business. I'm sure whatever deal he is offering is shady. Especially since he seems to hate Brandi so much. He says he always gives the families a good price, but I doubt that. His profit margin is way too high. By the time he sells land to me or anyone else, he only charges us at the low-end market rate to make his money. I ask him questions about how he gains the land for other deals, and he no doubt tells me lies. Now I'm thinking I'm part of the problem for not holding him account-able. I don't like the way that feels.

I'm going to do something about it.

"Mr. Ellis, I can help you solve your problem and keep Brandi happy too."

"How's that son, if you're so sure your friend is fleecing us?"

I don't miss the edge in his voice. "The land I buy with Byron are commercial spots that I renovate, but I've always wanted to develop a farm to table restaurant and a winery. I know Ma Kate's grape vines are still flourishing and you used to make and sell your own wine. You've got magnificent gardens and could expand them even more. With my expertise, we could make Edenton Shores a culinary destination."

"Humph. I'm listening." Ellis Growls.

"See, I could invest in your land, create the restaurant, and serve as your executive chef. I'd help you open it and hire your staff. We can split the profits 50-50, but you would own the land and I'd pay your family rent to lease it once my initial investment is paid back."

"Boy, are you serious? Now, don't play with me. I'm an old man and you know I don't take no charity."

I chuckle. "I'm very serious. This could be a win-win for all of us. It's not charity, Mr. Ellis. Like you said, I'm a businessman. I plan to make a lot of money out of this deal, but I want you to make even more. I want Brandi to be happy."

Mr. Ellis pauses for a minute. He's weighing his words. "I'm grateful for your offer. It sounds exactly like what we need, but I can't in good conscience say yes until whatever you and Brandi got going on is settled. I don't want you using this to get her. If she doesn't want you, then you need to let her go; even if I do, I think she'd be a fool to turn you away.

I laugh. "No sir, I'd never trick her that way. I'll talk to her, and we will come to an agreement. I won't even bring up what you and I have talked about. Then once she's decided about us, whether we're acquaintances, friends or lovers, we'll tell her about the restaurant idea. Does that work for you?"

"Yeah, that works for me. I got a feeling, the only option you're going to be happy with is lovers. But that's grown folks' business. You let me know when y'all got that all sorted out. You've got to the end of the month."

"Yes sir, I will."

"Good and tell that girl to call me. I ain't playing with her. I'll still tan her hide."

With that, he hangs up, and I shake my head in disbelief. That man will stay the same until the day he dies. I walk into my master bathroom suite and turn on the six body jets my black stone and marble shower provide. I'm invigorated, knowing that I have a solid plan to help Brandi and her family. I'd do anything to make her happy, and I know Edenton Shores means the world to her. She just needs to choose my brand of help.

She needs to choose me.

Chapter 11

No New Friends

Brandi

Where is the wine?

"Ciara, you don't understand. I need to be good and drunk before I see Riddick Kruger's sexy ass today. There's no way I'm starting my tailgating at his fraternity's tent. I'm pissed he even tried to put you up to it. He's doing the absolute most!"

I'm not his... yet.

She crosses her arms. "Pfft. No Brandi, he's not doing enough! Riddick is underestimating your stubborn ass. He will have to drag your dried-up pussy on to his dick."

The fact Riddick recruited Ciara in his efforts to see me today on his terms is cute but controlling. I probably should have answered his phone calls after he dropped me off last night. Honestly, I just wanted a hot bath and a cool bed after the events of the day. Riddick is overwhelming my senses. Usually, when a man gets all up in my space like he did last night; I'd cut him off before he got any more ideas in his head. But I can't cut off my best friend, and Riddick knows this! He's taking advantage of his rank in my life; I don't blame him. It's an excellent strategy. I just can't believe he turned my sister into a Benedict Arnold. She was going to deliver me to him on a silver platter!

I ignore her and keep walking towards the Rho Beta Chi tent.

Abbott Ridge College's Homecoming Tailgate is in full swing. You can hardly put your hands out to your sides, it's so packed. When you live in a small southern college town, homecoming is a big deal. The entire town comes out to celebrate the football team.

It is rather chilly, so I'm glad I went with the outfit I chose. I'm wearing my favorite Hudson jeans that make my ass look amazing. I have on a tight-fitting white Henley shirt that is magic when paired with my La Perla push-up bra. A Brown Gucci Belt and my custom-made Rho Beta Chi line jacket. I finished the look off with some cognac colored, four-inch thigh high Jimmy Choo Boots, a burgundy lip, and perfectly coiffed messy curls. *I look good.*

As if Ciara's reading my mind, she stops and looks me up and down with a narrowed gaze.

"What?" I ask with hands raised to the heavens. "Why are you staring at me?"

"Humph. I'm staring because I just realized how dressed up you are. Dressing nice for tailgating is not something you do. You always wear leggings so you can drink and eat with no restrictions. You want to look good for Riddick, don't you? Have you told me everything that happened at that step show? Something is up."

Hell no, I didn't tell you he gave me the best orgasm of my life with only his fingers in a public bathroom with the door slightly ajar.

"Ciara, nothing is up. I told you. He showed up backstage and kissed me. Then we had dinner at the Waffle House, and he said he wants to try a relationship. That's it."

I walk ahead, praying she will let it go. But I know better. Ciara can sniff an omission a mile away. She grabs me by the elbow and stops me. She looks in my eyes before grinning and talking a bit too loud. "Oh shit, you fucked him!"

"Shhhh!" I scramble and pull her to the side and away from people, which is nearly impossible. She finds this all gloriously funny.

"No, I didn't fuck him. He just... you know, made me come... a little. That's all."

Ciara's eyes widened. "What do you mean, that's all? Hell, if you ate carbs late at night it must have been one hell of an orgasm. I want details now!"

I sigh and go over the events in the backstage bathroom detail by detail, so she will leave me the hell alone about it. I end it by telling her I need a break from him, because it's all too much too soon. Ciara is incredulous at my response.

"What's too much too soon? Y'all have been friends for damn ever! He should have had your ass bent over somewhere screaming years ago."

I shake my head in disbelief. "Ciara, it's too much to think about explaining my feelings to my best friend of seventeen years. And he wants an answer now. It's a lot to examine. I blame him for this."

Ciara rolls her eyes and crosses her arms over her chest. "Brandi, how are you going to blame the man for giving you your first orgasm in over a decade? Your pussy is probably weeping with joy over the fact that she got some exercise. I wasn't sure the old girl would work the next time you cranked her up. Then that glorious, sexy, rich, South African man graciously swept the cobwebs out for you and declared his intentions to not only fuck you senseless, but to wife you! Girl, he did you a favor!"

I want to be mad, but she's so funny. My lips curl up. "You know what Ciara, you're no help! Just because you can go around fucking whoever you want without thinking about what it means doesn't mean we all can."

She feigns a Baptist fit and raises one hand to the heavens. "Oh, Saint Brandi, save me the drama, OK. What I do, and what you don't do, is far and in between. There is an ocean of difference in our sex lives. It's past time for you to get some, and if God sees fit to bless you with a man that we both know adores you; then that's a win-win. I would love for at least one man that I sleep with to understand me the way Riddick understands you."

We both stand there quietly. The moment has shifted, and neither one of us prepared for this level of introspection. For the first time, I look at my beautiful sister and I see a little sadness in her eyes. Eyes that usually dance with merriment or laughter have a levity in them. They're showing me that Ciara isn't as care-free as she pretends to be. She enjoys her escapades, but now I see that she's a mortal, just like the rest of us.

She wants companionship, love, and acceptance. She wants it all but has found no one worth wanting that with. I want that too; I just don't know if Riddick really does. He would never hurt me, but that's not enough for him to stay with me. Right now, he wants to make love to me, and he knows I won't take that lightly. I need to know that he wants to build a life with me. I want to be more than a best friend that he also likes to fuck. I want to be the love of his life. What if we have sex and he realizes he's not as enamored as he thought he was? Where would that leave our friendship? I don't know if I'm prepared to risk that.

"Ciara, I hear you, but this is a heavy conversation for a homecoming tailgate. Can we please get drunk now and show off how good we look to all our classmates?"

She pulls me into a hug. "Of course. Let's go."

We walk for a while and stop to nibble and sip at various tents. One fraternity had a barrel of something called oil that was delicious. But I had a feeling that if I had more than a cup of anything named oil, I wouldn't be able to walk, let alone drive, home.

When we get to the Rho Beta Chi tent, the barbeque smells divine. My sorors and I let Ciara mooch off our good graces and we both grab a full plate of ribs. I smile when I see Daphne. She rarely, if ever, comes to these things and I'm glad she's out. I walk over with my plate to speak with her.

"Daphne, hey girl, how did they get you to come out here?"

She laughs. "They promised me free liquor, so I was down. I'm so tipsy, I don't even know what's going on with the game."

"Girl, no one does. Look, I'm trying to get lit like you. I'll see you later, Ciara and I need to get drinks and catch up."

I look up and see Ciara heading to the cooler to grab us some drinks when she's stopped by the big, beautiful man that was at Daphne's shop, Seth Canton. I've got to admit the head of the Black Knights is fine as hell. He has skin the color of toffee and the height of a NBA basketball center. The black T-shirt and jeans he's wearing define his muscles and long lines. I don't even hate the leather vest he's rocking on top. And that smile is sinful. I can feel his presence from way over here... his power. I see why Ciara likes him, but I know my sister. She's one and done. This man is wasting his time.

I wait for her to flirt and then give him a light rebuke that will put him down gently. Once she's done, we can head back to the table and eat. Instead, her body becomes pliant, and her eyes are soft, looking up into his. Then he takes her hand, and she walks him to our table to sit down with his plate!

Who is this magical man, and what kind of spell did he cast on my sister?

I need to at least make sure he's not a criminal. I walk over, but a strong hand lands on my shoulder. The touch sends a chill through me, and I know it's Riddick. I weigh turning around until he whispers in my ear.

"Hey Kitten, have you been hiding from me?"

Motherfucker!

I turn and smile. "Hey... No, I just wanted to spend some time with Ciara before we linked up."

He arches an eyebrow and nods, acknowledging my bullshit. Then he looks up and gestures over to where Ciara and Seth are sitting.

"I see Ciara has met Seth. They seem cozy over there. Maybe that's why she didn't bring you to my tent like I asked. Mr. Canton distracted her."

I chuckle. "No, I told her I wanted to get good and drunk before I saw you. Don't worry, she gave it her all. I just didn't budge. So, wait, you know that man?"

Riddick nods. "Sure, we go way back. He's not from Abbott Ridge, but he's from two towns over in Waverly. Seth's a good dude. He lost his wife a couple of years ago to cancer and now he's a single dad."

My eyes fly open. "That man is a father? Isn't he the leader of some motorcycle gang?"

Riddick laughs and shakes his head. "Look at your bias shining through! I'm disappointed in you, Brandi. No, he's the leader of a motorcycle club. It's not much different from our fraternity and sorority. Just a bit more muscle. They keep the community safe."

I throw him a look of concern. "How do you know him?"

Riddick's lips turn up in an amused smile. "We robbed a bank together ten years ago. That's how I got the seed money for my restaurants."

I hit his shoulder when he burst out laughing. "Fuck you. I'm serious. That's my sister he's talking to."

"Ok, fine. I catered his mother's funeral repast a while ago. This was back when I used to take the food truck all around. He needed good and cheap food, because they barely had enough to bury her. I did it for free, and we've been cool ever since. Come on, let's go sit with them."

I don't want to barge in on whatever Ciara's got going on. If she wanted to wave me over, she would have. But I'm also not in a hurry to talk to Riddick about us, so this distraction is as good as any.

When we arrive, it takes Ciara a minute to even notice we're there. I catch her eye and give her a sly grin. *My, how the mighty have fallen.* She is really into this man. Seth stands and gives Riddick a hug, but I just silently tease my sister.

Riddick breaks the ice. "Ciara, I see we have a mutual friend. Seth, this is Ciara's sister and my best friend, Brandi Armstrong."

He leans over the table and shakes my hand. His grip is soft but freakishly strong. "Very nice to meet you, Brandi. Your sister has told me so much about you."

My eyebrows shoot up. "Has she now? Didn't y'all just meet yesterday?"

Riddick elbows me in the side, but I ignore him. Seth releases an easy laugh. "Yes, and can you believe she spent a good portion of our afterglow telling me how important you are to her?"

"*Afterglow... TMI.*"

"Umm Brandi," Ciara interrupts, "I was just telling Seth about the farmer's rights work you do. He was really interested in supporting your work."

He nods. "Indeed, I am. My family is from South Carolina, but they are all rice farmers down in Colleton County. I'd love to donate if that's appropriate. I'm also an attorney. I never took the North Carolina bar, but I'm sure I could do something around your office to help now and again."

I smile. "Are you trying to get on my good side, Mr. Canton?"

He laughs. "Of course. Is it working?"

I nod. "Yes, it is."

The four of us stay and talk for a while. I get so comfortable that I don't even notice when Riddick brings me another plate of food that I happily eat. This is over my daily calorie count. Usually, my skin would crawl, and I would have a high level of anxiety over it, but with Riddick's hand on my knee and warm gaze, I'm alright. His presence steadies me.

I turn to him. "I'm going to grab another glass of wine. Do you want anything?"

He shakes his half full Heineken. "No, I'm good. Do you want me to go get it for you?"

I smile. "No, you sit. I'll be right back."

Jumping up, I kick my leg over the picnic table bench and head for the makeshift wine bar. When I select a merlot, I hear a voice my mind won't let me forget.

"Red wine before 5 pm? It's too early for that Buttercup. You never know how to properly act, do you?"

Damn. Byron.

Chapter 12

No Fools

Brandi

NOT TODAY SATAN...

I turn around to face the devil head on because there's no other way to deal with lucifer.

It might be a little dramatic to call him that, but Byron Logan sure isn't goodness and mercy. I've kept him out of my line of vision, unless we're in a courtroom, for the better part of eighteen years. He doesn't want to see me and I sure as hell don't want to see him. So, I know he's only here talking to me now because he wants to be.

That is unsettling.

"Byron, your pretentious ass wouldn't know a cabernet from a merlot, so please save your words for someone who gives a damn." I step closer and poke my finger into the center of his chest as hard as I can. "And if you ever call me buttercup again; I'll cut your tongue out with a rusty letter opener. Got it!"

I turn away and continue to pour my wine, effectively dismissing him, but the jerk is still there.

I take a deep breath and prepare for whatever hell he's waiting to unleash. "Why are you here, Byron?"

He sets his mouth in a grim line and he looks me up and down. His leer makes me feel like I need a bath, and I don't like being assessed by him. "Brandi, I'm here because like you, I'm an alumnus of Abbott Ridge College. As you know, Rho Beta Chi is my sister sorority, and my brothers and I were invited to the tent for a meal. Thankfully, your sorors have more class and hospitality than you do. Now, I would like to get a glass of Chardonnay for my date, Mandy. If you don't mind."

He will not get a reaction out of me. This is what Byron always did, try to make me feel like an idiot. He acted like my first choice for college was silly. He insisted my plan to major in Environmental Science was a waste, and I listened. I love being a lawyer now, but he planted that seed in me because he was pre-law. Byron was convinced we would be powerful attorneys, thus thrusting him into politics one day. Even after he broke my heart, I followed his plan, because it was comfortable. Part of me also wanted to beat him at his own game. Do what he did, but better. *I did.*

Byron is a terrible litigator; that's why he moved to real estate and land rights law. I figure he just wants to make money and push paper. He likes to settle or bully his opponents out of court. But, I never bow. I make him fight me and my clients in court. We always win.

Thank God I'm not eighteen anymore. I'm wiser and if his behavior did not convince me before, I'm thoroughly persuaded now that he was a fool and a terrible lover. Riddick's three fingers did more than this jerk's dick ever did.

I plaster a fake smile on my face and gesture towards the wine bar. "Be my guest."

I walk away and vow to never see that jerk again unless we're in a courtroom. I'm so upset I don't pay attention to where I'm going. My inner monologue of hatred stops when I walk into a brick wall of good-smelling muscle. *Riddick.*

"What's wrong? What did he want?"

The look of concern on his face is endearing. He looks ready to kill whoever or whatever made me frown. Is it terrible I'm only now noticing how important his protective nature is to me?

Riddick always has my back, but I'm just now realizing that's something I want from my man.

Riddick is my man.

He has been my man for seventeen years. According to him, he will be my man for the foreseeable future. What am I so afraid of? This man is incredible, and he's all mine... *already.*

"He wanted nothing other than to insult me, of course. He says my choice of wine is inappropriate for the time of day." I laugh, but Riddick is already stomping over to where Byron is standing with Mandy.

What the hell is he doing?

When he reaches where they're standing, Byron visibly stiffens, and Mandy looks at him like he's a snack. *Byron's scared.* If Riddick was stalking towards me looking like The God of War, I would be scared, too. I rush over to prevent any bloodshed. Byron didn't really insult me. I didn't know Riddick would react like this. It was cute in my head, but violence is never OK.

This I don't need.

If a man says something inappropriate to me, I have enough agency to handle myself. I want to know my man has my back, but I don't need him to commit violence for my sake.

Riddick gets right in Byron's face and Mandy' simple ass is finally smart enough to walk away from the violence. "Stay the fuck away from Brandi. I will not tell your ass again."

When did he tell him the first time?

Byron shoots him that stupid smirk he employs when he's trying to project bravado. But I know he's pissing his pants right now. "I can talk, to her any time I want. You don't own her, no matter what you think."

I shudder at the words "own her." I mean, I'd never let Riddick dress me in a dog collar and call me his pet. But he sure as hell owns my pleasure. Shit, owning me isn't too far off.

Damn, I've got it bad.

Riddick snorts and steps even further into Byron's space. "You lost the right to talk to her the moment you broke her heart."

His words throw me into a state of shock. How does he know Byron broke my heart? Did Byron tell him? If Byron did, why didn't Riddick say anything to me about it? Have they been talking about me behind my back?

I step up and get in between the two of them. I turn to Riddick. "Wait, how long have you known that Byron and I used to be in a relationship?" Riddick snaps his eyes down to me and then they soften with worry. He didn't mean to let that slip, but now he's got to address it.

"He told me yesterday, Kitten, when we met for lunch, and I found out about his plans to buy Edenton Shores."

I nod. "Why didn't you say anything?"

He puts his hands in his pockets. "I figured you would have told me if you wanted me to know, and I didn't want to make you uncomfortable. You never have to explain yourself or your past to me."

Damn, I think I love him.

"Bullshit." Byron sneers. "As much as I would love to stand here and listen to this love fest between you two, I think I should shed some light on this situation. I told Riddick about us because he has some misplaced loyalty towards you, and it's costing us money. Edenton Shores is the perfect place for his new restaurant, and your grandfather is ready to sell. I thought if I let him know I had you and gladly dropped your ass; he'd realize you're not worth the trouble. But the more I think about it; you're not pretty enough to be his type. That's why he's never fucked you before. I think he's using you as an excuse to cut me out and get the land for himself. Because your wack ass sure ain't worth him giving up all the money he could make."

I hold Riddick back because I feel him jump. I can't let him hit Byron. He will never stop once he starts. He takes a deep breath. "Byron, if you don't stop lying and disrespecting Brandi, I'm going to have to kick your ass again."

I place my hand on my hip and shoot Riddick with an incredulous glare. "You kicked his ass?" *God, I wish I had seen that.* "Why didn't you tell me? That's cause for celebration!"

Byron answers. "He got a lucky punch in, that's all."

Riddick laughs. "If I punched you, you would have a broken nose and some more shit right now. What I did was almost choke your sleazy ass out. And I'll do it again if I see you're bothering Brandi. Or calling her out her name."

My mind is racing. Riddick choked Byron out and he's unbothered. Byron is still talking shit even though he knows he's beat. He's talking like he's not even really that worried about Riddick's threats. And when the hell did Byron call me out of my name?

What the hell went on in that meeting yesterday? Wouldn't Byron have emailed Riddick the balance sheets and specs of Edenton Shores before they met? Was Riddick really thinking about securing Edenton Shores for his new restaurant, like Mae said? Is there any merit in Byron's crazy ramblings? I know I'm not Riddick's normal supermodel type of woman, but his desire for me felt sincere. Maybe I'm missing something?

If Byron sent him the financial specs, why didn't he call me then so I would know the real financial state of the farm? Why wait?

I know how Byron works because I've had to defend so many clients against him in court; he always sends the financial specs to potential investors twenty-four hours before they talk about the venture. I can't imagine he would do anything different with Riddick.

Riddick knew how bad it was and said nothing. Instead, he told me to hear Mae out.

The hell?

I turn to walk away, and Riddick follows me. I don't acknowledge him.

Byron and Riddick secured six properties together. Their business relationship has always been a point of concern for me.

Something is shady and Riddick has some serious explaining to do.

I'd trust him with my life and I'm thinking about trusting him with my heart.

But can I trust him not to go after my family's land?

Chapter 13

No Disappearing Acts
Riddick

BRANDI IS WALKING AWAY...

That run in with Byron was not at all how I planned tailgating to go for Brandi and me. I wanted her happy, relaxed, and tipsy for stage two of my seduction campaign. Byron's presence created the opposite feelings, and I could kill him for making her so uncomfortable.

When I saw him approach her at the wine bar, I shot up from the picnic table Ciara, Seth and I were sitting on and headed over there. Ciara cursed under her breath when she saw him, and Seth asked if I needed any help. I told them I was good; I had a feeling of what Byron was telling her, and I would deal with it.

I wish I knew more about the dynamic of their past relationship. It feels like I'm stumbling in the dark with their hatred for each other. Any normal past relationship lacking serious trauma would not still contain this level of drama almost twenty years later. But Brandi won't talk to me about what happened and that hurts. It didn't before, but now that I'm thinking about us spending the rest of our lives together; the secrecy just won't do. I'm also convinced that whatever went down is the key to Brandi letting go and letting love rule in her life.

Her grandfather mentioned something about Mae being in

the middle of it all. I have some theories about his cryptic aside, but nothing set in stone. Byron is a selfish, arrogant wannabe. I always thought so. I never let on how much I was worth, because I didn't trust him. He and his family are in some dirty shit in town. What I know is that he's a domineering fool with the women he's dating. I've seen him go through quite a few and he likes his women quiet and submissive. Two things Brandi is not, and I doubt she ever was. I've never seen him put his hand on a woman, so I doubt physical abuse was a part of their relationship. If I ever found out it was, I'd have to kill him.

Now Byron talks like he has hold or ownership over her, and I'm disappointed that I never noticed the level of animosity he throws her way before. Now that I think about it, he was careful to hide his feelings toward Brandi. I should have known something was up. He was deceptively indifferent most of the time. But when he was at the restaurant with me, he seemed to be really nasty about his accusation of me thinking that Brandi was mine. That implies that he thought she was his. He was a little too gleeful to know that she hadn't been with anyone since him. Something just isn't sitting right, and now I want to know everything

I don't think he's a physical threat, but he makes Brandy uncomfortable. Then this past year, he asked about Brandi every time I saw him. His inquiries were possessive. I could tell that he didn't really care about her well-being. It seemed more like he was keeping tabs on her. He used to be frustrated because I never gave him much information. I just figured it was because he was trying to get a one up on his arch nemesis in court. I would have never guessed that she was his ex-fiancée.

I follow Brandi until we are walking side-by-side along the Perquimans River running through campus. I need to do damage control because I can feel the wheels inside Brandi's mind turning. She's wondering why I didn't tell her about the fight with Byron. She's also probably wondering how interested I really was about putting my restaurant at Edenton Shores. That's why she's so quiet. She's trying to decide what the truth is and what's a lie.

After the debacle with Byron, I told Ciara and Seth we were going for a walk. Warily, she came with me, but she's been silent. That stops now.

"How long were you and Byron engaged?"

She pauses by a tree and looks at me with an assessing frown. She's trying to decide whether she can get away with not answering my question. But after everything that's gone down the last two days, I think she knows she needs to talk to me. She looks away to gather some courage and then she blows out a long stream of air.

"We were engaged for three months, and it was the biggest mistake of my life."

I can't see her face, but I hear the regret in her voice. I want to ask what happened, but only fools rush in. Instead, I throw another benign question out.

"How old were you?"

They must have been extremely young. I wonder what even prompted them to think about tying themselves together for life at that age.

"I was eighteen and Byron was twenty. We were high school sweethearts. He was two years ahead of me, but we met at a NAACP meeting my sophomore year. Can you believe that Byron the barracuda used to style himself after a young Martin Luther King Jr.? He was more hardcore about Black farmer's rights than I was." She sighs. "I learned a lot from him, and then he broke my heart."

She finally looks back over at me. "You want to know what happened, don't you?"

I nod and walk closer to her. I take her hand to steady her breaths. She's nervous, but I want her to know that her secrets are always safe with me. "You never told me anything about Byron. Kitten, I was blindsided and I'm man enough to admit that I hated feeling like he had a part of you I didn't. I'm pretty sure he never deserved you. I was jealous and then a little angry that I never knew. The entire time I've dealt with Byron, he knew that you two were almost married. I talked about you and me as if no two people could be closer. I felt like a fool. But then he called you a bitch, and I had to choke him. Then I felt better."

Brandi laughs. "You can be so violent, Riddick. Remember that time you beat up that guy at the foam party for throwing suds in my eyes when I wouldn't dance with him?"

I squeeze her hand. "Of course, I do. I asked him nicely to apologize; he wouldn't, so he went home with a broken and bloody nose. I regret none of it. I'd fight an entire army of fools for you, Brandi. You know that."

"I do," she whispers. "I just don't know why. Why do you think I'm worth it when you could have any woman you desire?"

I stroke her face and place her hair over her right shoulder. "Because you're the only woman that takes my breath away with a single look. You're not only kind, but you're also impactful. You always leave communities better than you found them when you arrived. Family is important to you, and you wear your loyalty to your friends like a badge. You're well read and always impeccably dressed. Not to mention, you would never intentionally hurt anyone. Byron hates you because he sees the greatness in you, and it reminds him of his own mediocrity. You're the very definition of a sweetheart. Why wouldn't I choose you?"

A tear falls down her face. "You really see me, don't you?"

I place a kiss behind her ear. "Kitten, when you're around, I see no one else."

I look around and see too many people milling around for the conversation we need to have and the touches I want to give her. I grab her hand and pull her towards me.

"Come, I have a surprise for you." I tug her hand to move her forward, but she doesn't budge.

She narrows her eyes at me. "Where are you taking me?"

I waggle my eyebrows. "It's a surprise. Do you trust me?"

Offended, Brandi answers. "Of course, I trust you."

I pick up her hand and place a kiss on the inside of her palm. "I know, Kitten. Just checking... follow me."

We walk through campus and pass some of our old stomping grounds. When we come across the yard, or what some affectionately call the quad, we stop by our sorority and fraternity plots to take pictures. I always found it fascinating that the different cultures claimed the same space on campus as home base but gave it different names.

The students that ascribed more to Black American culture called this grassy area the yard. It was the place to see and be seen when I was in undergrad. It was also where each predominantly Black fraternity and sorority owned a plot that was painted with the organization's symbols and colors. No one stepped on the plots to sit or walk without being a member or having the expressed permission from a member. It was serious business.

I learned my lesson the hard way when I dared to walk across the Ques plot my freshman year. Being from South Africa, and White, I did not know who the Ques were or what a plot meant. They quickly apprised me of the knowledge, and I never made that mistake again.

Then you have the students that ascribe more to White American culture. They called this area the quad and treated it like an extensive park. They walked their dogs and threw Frisbees. They had picnic lunches and hosted outdoor games. It was also a place to be seen but was nowhere near as intense as the yard.

When you stepped onto the yard, you were dressed to impress. If you were coming to the quad, you could be dressed in your pajamas, and no one would look twice. Brandi helped me navigate all the American cultural norms when I arrived and she's a big reason I pledged my fraternity. I'm one of the few White men in Psi Kappa Chi, but I love the Black American heritage and I serve the community with pride.

Once we reach Walter Hall, Brandi squeals. "OH, my gosh, our old dorm! I haven't been inside in years!"

I wink. "I still have some pull, and since they are still renovating this building, I got permission for us to go inside your old room." I climb a few steps and then reach down to grab her hand. "Ready?"

Brandi smiles and takes my hand.

I'm ready for anything.

Chapter 14

Yes, Surprise Me
Brandi

Riddick's surprise makes me reminisce...

Walter Hall, on Abbott Ridge's college campus, was my home for four years. I never wanted an apartment, and much to my grandfather's chagrin, I refused to move back to the farm. I knew if I did, it would be too tempting to cut Mae in her sleep.

Instead, dorm life suited me just fine. Once Ciara came of age, she was my roommate, and we ruled the dorm like the Queens we are. We both loved the camaraderie of both the males and females on our floor. It never occurred to us that a co-ed dorm was a privilege until we talked to our other friends from high school that attended Historically and Black Colleges and Universities in our state like North Carolina A&T or North Carolina Central. Once we talked to them, we found out that a co-ed dorm was a privilege for honor students or a giant taboo all together. That was almost twenty years ago, so things may have changed by now.

One constant of the four years that I stayed at Walter Hall was my nightly dreams of Riddick. He was the Resident Assistant the entire time I lived there. I think he only stayed because I did. He sure as hell didn't need the work-study money. I knew Riddick Kruger was loaded. Whether he would admit it was an entirely different matter.

Riddick never flaunted his wealth. He never threw it around to impress anyone. His wealth was subtle. For example, he never ever complained of not having money for something. The broke college student trope did not apply to him. Whether it was a meal, books or something random, like a concert ticket, he always had money to cover himself and everyone around him. I honestly can't remember one meal or activity that Ciara and I ever shelled out our own money for. I hate charity, but he would pay with such cool grace that you felt guilty denying him the opportunity to give.

His car wasn't anything flashy, like a Mercedes or a BMW, but it was expensive. It wasn't the Range Rover; it was the Land Rover Discovery, and he tricked it out with every off roading ancillary you could think of. Many people didn't know that it was a signature of understated wealth. His tastes came from his South African roots. His parents own a game reserve, for Christ's sake! I'm sure an off-roading vehicle was the family car.

Last, Riddick stayed impeccably dressed. For him, it wasn't about logos or names. It was about luxurious fabrics. Some of the wannabe rich guys on campus might have the new Ralph Lauren sweater or even a sweater made by Hugo Boss or Gucci. But Riddick had rows and rows of cashmere sweaters stacked in his drawers. His shoes were Italian leather, and the man's jeans were soft as silk. Then there's the way he smelled. He did not wear the mass-produced Chanel Bleu or Dior Homme. Riddick wore a curated fragrance by Tom Ford.

I went to Neiman Marcus with him once to have a bottle mixed, and my jaw dropped when he casually swiped his card for $800. Over time, all the little things added up, and I realized—*OH, he's rich*. I also realized he could have gotten an apartment anytime he wanted to, but he didn't. He stayed and kicked it in hot ass Walter Hall with Ciara and me.

Knowing that fine ass man stayed two doors down from me while I was sleeping naked and sweaty in my bed was enough to send me over the edge of pleasure every night. I'd be mortified if he knew the things, I wanted him to do to me repeatedly in this very dorm room.

Now he's brought me here, and not only are we here, but he also decorated the room with flowers, candles and the scent of vanilla.

This is the great seduction, and I'm here for it, mind, body and soul. I will live out my fantasies and figure the rest out later.

Holding his hand, I turn to Riddick and clear my throat. "What's all this?"

He drops my hand and peels off my line jacket, laying it on the twin bed. His hands rest on my arms and slowly rub up and down, giving me goosebumps and shivers of pleasure. There's nothing else like his touch in all the world. Eventually, my breathing matches the pace of his hands. He's controlling the tempo of my breath with his touch.

What kind of sorcery is this…?

"Kitten, did you know this moment is my fantasy in real life? Even though we were best friends; I used to dream about coming over here and licking every inch of your delicious body all night long. My thoughts made me feel bad because I knew you were just my friend. That's why I never acted on it. I couldn't disrespect you that way. But today, I'm hoping we're in a different place and that you'll let me show you how good a lover I can be."

I'm smile so hard I'm afraid I might pull a muscle. Could it be? He was having the same fantasies I was all those years ago. It sounds too good to be true. Now that I know he had the same desires I had; the expectations for this moment are higher. It needs to be magical, but I'm not Houdini.

I haven't had sex in almost two decades.

I don't want to let him down. *All those years with not so much as a kiss.* Now I realize how crazy it sounds. Do I even know how to make love anymore? What if I embarrass myself? I mean, what if I'm so bad that he can't even go through with it?

The more I think about this, the more it feels like a bad idea.

There must be a way to put this off a little longer until I can get my wits about me.

Riddick narrows his eyes and studies me while my mind races. A look of Aha crosses his features and he crouches down a bit to wrap his hand around the back of my head. Pulling our foreheads together, he swoops in to erase my fears like a sexy knight in shining armor.

"Easy there, Brandi. What's going through that beautiful mind of yours? You locked up on me."

I close my eyes. I can't talk to him when he's this close; his stare is way too intense. His smell is way too intoxicating. I want to kiss every inch of him and run away in equal measure. Riddick gently nudges my eyes open with a brush of his finger under my chin. I look up and confess everything.

"Riddick, I thought we were coming here to continue talking. Now it seems like there's going to be a lot more going on than talking. Honestly, I don't know if I'm ready for that." I close my eyes again and whisper, "It's been a very long time."

Riddick pulls me close against his chest and rubs up and down my spine. "Hey, hey wait a minute. My Kitten does nothing she's not ready for. If you're not ready for me to take that sweet body captive in pleasure, that's OK." He winks and plants a kiss on my forehead. "If all you're ready to do is talk about what happened with Byron years ago; I'm here. We will sit on this bed, and I'll hold you through it. If that's all that happens today, I'm good with that. Either way, before we start, can I give you a present first?"

I laugh and pull away from him and gesture to the candles and flowers. "So, you mean this isn't my present? Because I've got to tell you, this is smooth Kruger."

Soundlessly, he picks me up and I yelp. Then he deposits me on the bed. "No, this is not your present." He scoots down and pulls a large Marigold colored box from under the bed. When I see the navy-blue letters spell out Louis Vuitton on top, my heart stops for a second. "This is your present."

Riddick knows how much I love Louis Vuitton. He also

knows how often I buy it for myself. It's my reward. Being a farm rights advocate is not lucrative by any means, but I do alright. Especially when the legal fees kick in from the corporations and investors that represent them, like Byron Logan. I get an innate sense of pleasure knowing that fool pays all my client's legal fees every time he loses a property to me in court. He's basically paying a portion of my salary, and I enjoy taking his money. Every year, I buy myself a bag or two to remind myself that I'm worth the luxury. I learned early to normalize luxury in my life. I should have normalized pleasure as well. Then I wouldn't have anxiety attacks when a sexy man like Riddick kisses me senseless.

I rub my hand over the box and look up. "Riddick, you didn't have to do this."

He sits next to me and rubs a hand over my hair like I'm a precious gift to admire. "Hmmm, I know you think whatever is in that box is something you can get for yourself, which may be true, but I still wanted to get it for you. Because you're worth me trying to impress you."

I fight a tear falling. "Riddick, I don't think anyone understands me half as much as you do, and I'm grateful for it."

He plants a quick kiss on my forehead before fingering the ribbon wrapping the box. "Take a look."

I take a deep breath and lift the top off the box and dig into the tissue paper until I see something that makes me squeal with glee. It's a special addition mirrored Louis Vuitton Neverfull GM from the 2008 Marc Jacobs Collection. They only made 100 in this style, and it looks brand new.

"Oh, my gosh Riddick! Where did you find this?"

Riddick chuckles. "It wasn't easy, but I know it's your unicorn because you talk about it all the time. One finally went up for auction at Sotheby's London. I've had a sales alert activated on my account for over seven years. When one finally came on the market, I won the auction. It's all yours, kitten."

I run my fingers over the bag. "Riddick, I know this bag cost you somewhere north of $20,000. I don't even know if I can take this."

Riddick shakes his head. "You let me worry about how much it costs. I wouldn't buy anything I couldn't afford. You, darling, are priceless, so nothing is too expensive for you. I want you to enjoy it. You can wear it every day or put it up in your closet and look at it behind a glass case. Whatever gets your rocks off."

I jump up off the bed and throw my arms around his neck and kiss him until we're both panting and breathless. This man is incredible. He listens to me. Not just the important stuff, but the whimsy too. I can't believe he remembered how much I wanted this bag. Something in my chest moves away, and I think it's fear. I'm no longer afraid of today's interaction; I'm hopeful.

He kisses me back, and it increases with intensity as my courage grows. Fuck my fears. Fuck the years I've wasted drowning in my past. I want to be free. I don't know how far I'll go today on this journey of passion, but I'm not turning away before we even begin.

I climb on top of Riddick and straddle him, never breaking our kiss. His hands immediately grab onto my ass and squeeze. I smile against his lips.

"Riddick Kruger, you really are an ass man, aren't you?"

He chuckles and leans back, dragging me on top of his body. "I'm a Brandi's ass man. I've dreamed about biting, licking, and eating out your fat ass since freshman year."

His filthy words spark another level of bravery inside me. I pull away from his lips and drag his shirt up his body. Hard muscle sculpts his massive chest. Beautiful tattoos adorn it. The scattering of soft black hair down his stomach leads me down a happy trail to his dick. Hesitantly, I reach out to run my hand down the soft skin with a light touch. He hisses.

"Touch me, Kitten. Touch me as much as you want."

So, I do.

I rub my hands over his stomach and massage his taut muscles. When my hands have enough, I use my tongue. My licks are soft and furtive at first; ironically, like a kitten lapping up a bowl of milk. He tastes salty and sweet at the same time, and I become hungry for more of him.

He doesn't make a sound when I unbuckle his jeans and slowly slide them down his raised hips. His hands reach down and gently stroke my hair as I rub my hands all over his hips and down his hard length through his black boxer briefs. He's incredibly sexy and I'm incredibly turned on.

I lift my head, and our eyes meet. Tapping the waistband of his boxers, I whisper, "May I?"

His smirk is naughty. "May you what Kitten?"

I bite my bottom lip and think of what to say. I may as well keep it as real and filthy as he does. I've read enough romance novels to dirty talk with the best of them. "May I roll down your boxers and pull out this giant dick? I want to suck you, and make you come until you are bone dry."

His eyes flash with dangerous desire, and I'm taken aback. "Are you sure?" His voice hitches at the end. His control holds on by a thread. "You know we don't have to do anything, and I'll still enjoy our time together."

"Yes Riddick, I'm sure. I really, really want to suck your dick. I need to. Please…"

Am I begging?

His jaw clenches, but his eyes remain soft. "Then do it Brandi. But suck me hard. After so many years of waiting, I don't want to wait to come down your pretty throat any longer."

I suck in a breath and nod before pulling his dick out and wrapping my hand around the hard length. It's beautiful in a way that only a stiff cock can be. It's strong and covered in soft skin, with purple veins pulsating in angry need. I try not to think about how I'm going to get what must be at least ten hard inches down my throat. *But I will.*

I stay on my knees but lean over in a deep arch to place the ass he loves so much in the air.

My tongue swirls around the bulbous tip, and he lets out a

deep grunt. He inhales deeply when I lick him again. *I want more.* I lick the pre-cum leaking from the tip and moan in delight. He tastes like mine… *finally.*

I continue to lick from the base of his balls all the way up his shaft. His hand tightens in my hair, and I know it's time to go to work. I try not to think about it being a job I haven't done in a very long time. Instead, it's the first day of a new career of love and passion that I've worked hard to get.

One thing the 200 or so Mafia romances I've read taught me over the years is that men like you to take them deep into your mouth, and that's what I'm going to do. I want Riddick undone and panting on this bed, much like he unraveled me in that backstage bathroom. I lean over and take his length into my mouth, licking the sensitive underside of his length as he goes down. Once he hits the back of my throat, I gag and spit in shock. But Riddick takes over and I feel a sense of calm when he places his gentle hand firmly on my jaw and looks down at me.

"Relax your throat, Kitten. I'm coming down again." And he does. With my hair firmly in his grasp, he thrusts his hips up while moving my mouth up and down over his dick. The groans he releases are music to my ears.

"Fuck Brandi. That pretty mouth of yours is perfect around my cock. That's it baby, suck and swallow me all the way down your delicate little throat."

With each thrust, I take another inch. He pulls out to let me breathe before slamming into my mouth again. It becomes a sloppy wet punishing rhythm and I'm lost in the pleasure of it all. My pussy is aching, and I hate I didn't slip my jeans off first. No matter, I reach between my legs and over the wet fabric with hard circles to release some of the pressure, and it takes the edge off.

Riddick's thrusts come faster, and I know he's about to explode.

"Kitten, I'm coming."

He's warning me in case I don't want to swallow, but there isn't anything I'd rather do in this moment. I take control and hollow my cheeks to suck him harder as he pushes up and into my mouth. After two more strokes, the warm cum shoots down my throat. My pussy convulses while my fingers continue to rub my crotch. Riddick releases a roar that is primal, and I enjoy every decibel. *My God, this is hot.*

I clean his dick with my tongue and sit up to look at him with panting breaths. He reaches up and grabs the back of my head to pull me down into an open mouth kiss. When we come up for air, he sits up and pulls me into his arms, rocking me slow. We stay silent for a while, but then he speaks.

"I love you, Brandi."

Chapter 15

Yes, You Love Me

Riddick

LOVE, tell me what happened...

I'm driving Brandi home fully satisfied and ready to move forward. She rode to the tailgate with her sister, but apparently Ciara is busy with Seth. *I'm grateful.* Brandi doesn't need an excuse to run away and hide from me or us like she did last night. Ciara can't rescue her from the feelings that rushed in after our dorm room tryst and my declaration of love.

The interlude in her old dorm room is still fresh in my mind. We laid in the bed and cuddled until the sun went down. We were light and carefree until Brandi noticed her phone didn't chime with notifications from Ciara and a frown settled on her face. She got antsy.

I assured her Ciara knew of my surprise plans for her, so she wouldn't worry. However, Brandi worried she was off gallivanting with Seth; a man she barely knew. How can she be safe with a man that runs a fringe motorcycle club? She exclaimed that he's a vigilante, not boyfriend material. I tried to explain to her that both things can be true. She wasn't having any of it. Once I got Ciara on the phone for her, she settled down.

"She's the only sister I have," she tried to explain as we packed up the room.

"I know, Kitten. But Ciara is a grown woman. You're going to have to let her find her own way."

She nodded, and we headed out to find food. Now we're driving home.

I break up the thoughts of worry that are likely still lodged in her mind. "Why don't you tell me about your engagement to Byron? It will take your mind off Ciara." *And the way you just sucked me down like a champ.*

She nods and starts from what I assume is the top.

"I met Byron when I was fifteen years-old at a young NAACP meeting. Immediately, I thought he was the smartest guy I'd ever met. He quickly became my everything, and I fancied myself in love."

She pauses and closes her eyes like that's the end of the story. I shift in the seat of my Tesla. Hearing her declare her love for another man fills me with a soft rage. I know it's ridiculous to be jealous of her past, but I can't help it. I want her to feel that way about me. She exhales, signaling she's ready to continue.

"My grandparents never let me date, but because Byron was a Logan, they made an exception. We were together my sophomore through senior year, and he was a year ahead of me. I always wanted my first-time having sex to be important. It was one of the last pieces of advice my mother gave me before she died. I told Byron this repeatedly, but he wouldn't let up about us having sex. He did everything in his power to convince me he was special enough and then in my senior year, I gave my virginity to him and that's when things changed."

"He became controlling. Ciara hated him and he could not stand her. He tried to make it seem like Ciara was jealous of me and I hate to think what would have happened if I'd stayed with him longer than I had. He was so image conscious and determined to make us a power couple, even when we were 18 and 20. I thought he only wanted what was best for us. Now I know he was abusive."

"Anyway, when it was time to make my college decision; I chose Spelman College."

I look at her. "Wait, I never knew you wanted to go to Spelman. I could see you loving it there with all those amazing Black women changing the world."

She chuckles. "Boy, what do you know about Spelman College?"

I wink. "You forget, I own two very popular restaurants and wineries in Atlanta. I know everything about any city I invest in. You can't know Atlanta without knowing about Spelman and Morehouse College."

She smiles. "I see. But yes, I had an acceptance and scholarship to Spelman, but Byron was adamant against me going. By that time, he was a sophomore at Abbott Ridge and wanted me there with him. I refused, but he just kept badgering; talking about the future we were supposed to share, changing the landscape of Black farming. So, he proposed to get me to stay. I said yes, because I thought I was in love, and he promised me the entire world."

Brandi wrings her hands and sucks in a harsh breath. My heart aches for her.

"Three months later, I went to the barn to brush and ride my horse Sadie and I caught him fucking Mae in the hay."

It's a quiet moment before I sneak a look to my right. When I see Brandi's tears, I squeeze her knee.

"So that's why you hate Mae?"

Brandi snaps her head in my direction with a mild look of open-mouth shock. "I don't hate Mae. She's my cousin Riddick. I could never truly hate my family."

I slip her a side-eye. "You could have fooled me, Kitten. You always assume the worst about her. Brandi, you say nothing nice about Mae. And now that I know why, I understand all the little verbal jabs you've thrown her way over the years. I knew she must have done something to you. I just didn't know what.

The Wine Down

Constantly, you are reminding her of what I'm sure she believes is her worst moment. You hold back forgiveness like it's your right to be bitter. If that's not hate, then I don't know what is. The thing is, I know you. I know how much and how hard you love. I believe you love your cousin, but you act like you hate her. It's time for how you feel and how you act to line up."

The tears fall down her face in a race to her soft lips. I hate to make her cry, but it's time for Brandi to let the past go. If she's free; she will love. I've learned through my own family drama that unforgiveness only breeds sickness, mistrust, and self-loathing. No one wants to be bound up by past hurts. We must find the courage to set ourselves free. A good cry is a great place to start.

"Riddick." Her voice is so soft I almost miss it. I stop at the red light and turn to her. "Mae asked me to forgive her once. And I wouldn't. She had just had Toya, and she told me that Byron would show up at her job and tell her all these things while we were together. He made her feel special and told her so many lies about how I felt about her. He told her I planned to take over the farm and cut her out. That I was interested in farm rights because I wanted to know the law so I could take over. He played her against me and by the time she fucked him, she felt like I deserved it. He mind-fucked her so bad, and she felt horrible for falling for it. She was distraught with remorse. But I was still so mad! I told her I would never forgive her, and she should save her words. We were never the same after that. We've built a giant wall between the two of us, and I don't know if we will ever be able to scale it."

I shake my head. "You don't have to scale it, Kitten. Just tear it down."

She sucks in a breath. "You're right. I know it's up to me now. And I'll do it. I don't hate Mae. I don't know if I ever did. The hurt was just so big. I give my trust to very few, so once you lose it, it's damn near impossible to get it back."

She speaks of trust. I need to talk to her about the true financial state of the farm and how her grandfather and I propose to fix it. She won't like it, but I don't want her to think I'm keeping anything from her. I don't want her to think I have designs on her family's property. But we're making progress right now and I don't want to ruin it by talking about Edenton Shores.

I'll tell her tomorrow.

"Thank you for sharing that, Brandi. Why didn't you tell me before? I would never have been friends on any level with Byron if I knew how terribly he did you. Fraternity brother or not, he's not a good man. Know I would have never chosen his word over yours."

She shrugs. "I guess I was embarrassed. After the break-up, I was a mess. I developed a minor eating disorder and anxiety. I altered my future for a man that convinced me we were in love. I didn't want you to know I was weak."

I pull into her driveway and park. "I'd never think you were weak Brandi. You're just human. Tell me, though, why did you abstain from sex for so long. How is all that connected?"

"Well, I always felt I wasted my first time, and that sex clouded my judgement. In my mind, if I never had sex, I couldn't be duped again. I couldn't be swindled into love and have my life turned upside down."

"Hmm, I see. You know you're putting too much pressure on yourself about your first-time. Sex is whatever you make it. You place the importance on it, it does not place it upon you. Byron was a jerk, but you loved him. That's Ok. Take the good from that memory and move on. Sex did not cloud your judgement; a fool lied to you and cheated. That's all. Your life is much bigger than that break-up."

"Thank You Riddick."

I grab her hands and kiss her knuckles. "I'm just telling the truth, Kitten. You have too much life to live than to be bound by that horrible man and relationship. He's inconsequential. Now…

Speaking of living your life. May I come inside? I'd love to get started on the rest of your life."

She doesn't hesitate. "Please do. I need to make up for some moments of pleasure."

I turn the car off and unbuckle her seatbelt. She jumps out and I follow her up the drive. As we approach her porch, we notice a man lying in her hammock. Just when I grab and toss her behind me, the man stands up. It's Ellis, Brandi's grandfather.

I release her, and she moves towards him. "Granddad, what are you doing here?"

He gives her an angry glare. *He's pissed.*

"Well, since you wouldn't answer my calls, I thought I better show up here to talk to you." He looks my way. "Have you told her yet?"

Brandi looks at me for answers. "Told me what?"

Shit. It's only been twelve hours. Why is he here?

Her grandfather spits tobacco into a can he carries. Then cuts me off before I can even speak. "About how he's going to save our farm by putting his new restaurant at Edenton Shores."

Brandi turns to me and scowls. "What? So, you are planning to take our land and build another stupid restaurant?"

Fuck.

"No Brandi… I mean yes… I mean I talked with your grandfather this morning about building a restaurant on the land. But it's not what you think. He came to me for help, and this was the best option. You will keep ownership of the farm. My restaurant will be your tenant. I'll be paying you."

"Oh sure, and what happened today in the dorm room had nothing to do with you trying to butter me up so you can use Edenton Shores? I should have known it was all bullshit."

Ellis stands a little taller. "What's this about a dorm room?"

Taking a deep breath, I silently name the 54 African countries alphabetically to calm down. How can she come at me like this? She should know I'd do nothing to hurt her. Everything I do, or have ever done concerning her, was to spare her any pain.

"Brandi. Your grandfather called me today trying to find you. He told me what was going on, and I came up with the idea on the fly. I know how much ownership is important to you, so I made it work, and this way the farm would be safe from blood-suckers like Byron."

She laughs.

Fucking. Laughs.

"Oh, don't act all high and mighty. You've been doing business with that bloodsucker for years. I know Byron sent you the farm balance sheet before you met with him yesterday. When you saw the farm was in dire trouble, why didn't you come to me and tell me? This is what I do. I fight and save farms. Instead, you feed me some bullshit about Mae, and I fought with my cousin. You don't love me, no man does. You just wanted to fuck me; and you almost did. I'd be so gone over you, I wouldn't mind you coming in to swoop in and steal our land right from under us."

Now she's screaming, and I can't hold back anymore. I walk over and grab her, trying to get her to look at me. But her grandfather steps over and taps my shoulder, telling me to let her go. Reluctantly, I obey and turn away to rub my hand through my hair. This is un-fucking-believable!

"Granddaughter," Ellis rumbles while taking her arms in a firm grip. "You've got it all wrong on two accounts. First, I asked Riddick for help. The farm can't run the same way it has; it's just not profitable. What he offered to do for us would let the Armstrong's' keep our land and we'd make more in one year from his rent and 50% of his restaurant profits than we do with two years of crops."

Brandi's eyes widen and her voice softens. "50% of your restaurant profits…? Riddick, you offered that?" Oh, now she wants to be reasonable. She knows I don't play with my money, but she also should know I don't play when it comes to her. Do our seventeen years of friendship mean nothing to her?

I don't turn around or say a word. I'm on Mali alphabetically, and still not calm enough to speak to her.

Her grandfather continues. "And that boy loves you. He told me himself, but he didn't have to. I've watched how he's held you together all these years and given you unconditional love and friendship when his heart was hurting. Anybody with eyes could see that he was in love with you, but he put his feelings aside to make sure you were comfortable and OK. He loved you the way you needed it and didn't ask you for anything in return. Now I'm not saying you got to be with him-but that's genuine love, Brandi and that kind of love doesn't come around every day. I came here to tell you about the plan and get you on board. But I see you just as stubborn as I am. But I need you to be OK with this, because it's not just about me and you, it's about what's best for our entire family. Riddick's plan is a godsend, and we need to take it."

Ellis Armstrong slaps my back before he walks down the steps and gets in his truck. I don't know how we missed it before. I hear Brandi shifting from foot to foot, and I know she's nervous. Good, she should be. What she accused me of was terrible. I know I needed to tell her, but I never thought she'd think that badly of me.

"Riddick, I'm sorry... I just... I don't know. Will you please turn around and talk to me?"

I don't turn around. Instead, I tap my foot and continue to calm down.

Uganda... Zambia... Zimbabwe. OK, I'm ready.

I turn and see the worry on her face. She really is sorry, but that's not enough. I need her to be mine, so she never feels insecure about us or my motives again.

"Your book club retreat is tomorrow, correct?"

She nods.

"Good. Meet me at Antonio's when it's over. We'll talk then."

"But Riddick..." she protests, but I raise my hand to silence her. I can't talk right now.

I want to reach out and hug her. I crave to reassure her, but that's not what she needs right now. She needs to feel uncertain, even if for a day.

I turn and walk down the steps, get into my Tesla, and drive away. When I look in the rearview mirror, she's still hugging herself on the porch, and I almost turn around.

Don't worry Kitten, Tomorrow, it will all make sense.

Sunday: The Book Club Retreat

One who perseveres has no misfortune.
-South African Proverb

Chapter 16

Yes, Take Me

Brandi

ONE MORE HOUR *until it's time to go...*

My mind rarely wanders during book club meetings. I'm the leader and stay mentally all in. Today, however, I'm all over the place.

Riddick's haunting last words yesterday left me sweating like a pig in July.

I've worked on this retreat all year and I'm barely present. My sisters asked me more than once what's on my mind, but I deflect and deny. If they had any idea that I allowed Riddick to make me come inside a public bathroom at the Abbott College gymnasium, or that I sucked his dick in my old dorm room, or that I accused a man that's loved me unconditionally of trying to fuck me for my land; that would effectively end the meeting.

I think it's best if they think nothing's changed between me and my best friend.

I hope he's still at least my best friend.

My book club sisters already smell blood in the water over the whispers of him showing up and staring at me like I was the last piece of meat at a BBQ backstage on Friday. Mandy complained to anyone willing to listen. The last thing I need is my sorors marrying us off and picking out bridesmaids' dresses in their heads before I even know what he's going to say at Antonio's today.

Personal drama aside, the book club retreat is going off without a hitch. Our member Shannon's bed-and-breakfast, The Inn at Abbott Ridge, perfectly catered the food. I stayed at the inn one weekend last year for a staycation and all I remember about that weekend was the amazing meals and wine. I knew we would eat her food at this year's retreat. She rose to the occasion. In celebration of our October book selection, *Craving a King*, she went with a West African inspired menu.

At first, I was nervous about her endeavor into African cuisine. It's not every day an American woman from the south who can't show you Accra on a map, takes on Jollof rice. But she did, and Shannon crushed it. Her chale sauce was perfectly blended, and the rice was nice and loose the way I prefer.

I may be from North Carolina, but my grandmother's people are from the Sea islands in South Carolina. Lowcountry folks don't play with their rice, so I grew up a connoisseur. The low country Gullah and Geechee people are descendants of the West African people brought to America in chains. The cuisine was one of the few things not stripped from them and it still reigns deliciously supreme today. I set my bar high for this menu, and she met it. The meat pies were crispy and flaky on the outside and full of soft, flavorful shrimp, pork, or chicken on the inside. And she did not shy away from scotch bonnet peppers for the stews. Between that and the curated wine bar, the Meet Cute Book Club was in heaven.

Daphne and her team created temporary tattoos of every member's favorite book for the swag bags I insist upon every year. I want our members to leave with keepsakes that make them feel loved and a part of something special. Our sister Mila Santos graciously gifted every member a $20 gift card to her bookstore Books and Beans, and the squeals of joy were genuine. I am grateful for the way we support each other and give. Our book club is about more than reading steamy novels and hoping for our own happy endings. While our sorority is about more than stepping and service. It's about sisterhood most of all.

"My last thought on this book is that kings come in all flavors, and I should try to taste them all."

I snap out of my fog when I hear my soror Catherine March. She begged for a royal romance as the October pick. I picked a royal romance, but not one of the Prince Charles and Princess Diana variety. I'm curious to hear her thoughts after reading it.

"I learned so much about the Ashanti and Ghana. I never knew about the royalty there and I honestly think King Kofi Ajyei may be the sexiest sovereign I've ever read about. He had me hot and bothered all night long! Especially when I added the Audible narration..." Catherine fans herself. "That male narrator was HOT!"

I snicker. She's right. The audiobook is even better. I'll take Uduyak's West African accent over a British one any day of the week. Catherine turns to me and smiles.

"Thank you for pushing our boundaries, Brandi. I will read more Black romance authors. I don't know what took me so long."

I nod and smile. "I'm happy your Kindle library will gain some color. Plus, that gives you even more books to sift through."

Mission accomplished. Our sorority is diverse, and our book selections should be too.

I clap my hands and stand. "Alright ladies, Catherine gave us our last words on *Craving a King*. Don't forget to pick up November's pick, Brutal Vows by J.T. Gessinger, soon! That meeting will be virtual. Now it's time to drink and be merry!"

My sisters clap and stand, dispersing to the bar and snack table to eat and catch up. They all take a moment to tell Daphne and me how well we did. I hang around for thirty more minutes before I step outside and practically run to my car.

I don't know why I'm so excited to get to what I am sure will be an awkward conversation with Riddick, but I am. I want to see him, regardless of what's in front of us. He's likely not as pressed to see me after what went down yesterday, but I pray he's calmed down. I don't know why I said the things I did. I was just scared. Riddick sent me the proposal last night, and he really is saving Edenton Shores. *He's saving my family.* There was no message or note of comfort with the delivery, just the attachment.

I have a nagging feeling that he only wants to clear the air today. I imagine Riddick frequently commands women to come all over his hand and suck his dick, in all kinds of places. He's a player. A sweet, loveable one, but a player all the same. After my display yesterday, he may feel I'm not worth the drama. I've got to keep my head on straight and not fall further in love with my best friend. That could ruin us.

I throw all my sensible thinking to the wind when I step outside and spot Riddick leaning against his Tesla. *God, the man looks like sex on a huge stick.* He's dressed in all black, like the Omen, and his hair is loose with a lock falling over his forehead. His massive forearms are crossed against his powerful chest and his legs are crossed at his ankles. He's swag and sauce in a bottle, and he looks like he's waiting to do more than talk to me. His smirk is lethal, and my pussy has already betrayed me. I shake my head and go to him.

What is he doing here?

I needed a bit more time. I planned to use the car ride to prepare and face him. Now I'm thrown off center… *again.*

I barely contained my annoyance when I confront him. "Riddick, I thought the plan was for me to meet you at Antonio's when this meeting was over?" I shoot him a glare, but I don't possess enough anger to mean it. He knows this and his face cracks into a grin that takes over his entire toasted almond face. *He is so beautiful.*

He reaches out and takes my hand and squeezes. "The more I thought about that plan, I didn't like it. I didn't want you to overthink and weasel your way out of our meeting because you think I hate you or something. I know how that mind of yours works. So, I thought I would make it easier for my kitten and escort you to our destination."

Does this mean we're still friends? Are we more?

I narrow my eyes. "Riddick, I would not bail. And I am more than capable of getting to Antonio's on my own."

He reaches up and runs his thumb across the corner over my mouth like he's wiping crumbs away. But there's no crumb, just my scorching skin reacting to his touch. "I know. You can do anything Brandi. You're incredible. But we're not going to Antonio's."

I scrunch my face in confusion. "What are you talking about? Antonio's is our favorite spot."

He nods and rubs my cheek. "Yes, it was. But it's a new day for us Brandi, it's time for a new spot. Don't you think so?"

I can't breathe. What does he mean by a new day? Three days ago, I didn't want a new day. I wanted the days we always have. I still do. *Don't I?* Why am I rubbing my cheek up against his hand like a purring kitten? He keeps petting me and I like it. My eyes close at his touch while I listen to him tell me his plans for us this evening.

"I thought you might like to see my new restaurant, *Busu,* in Raleigh. Do you know what Busu means in Swahili?"

I shake my head.

He smirks. "It means kiss." He plants a soft kiss on the corner of my mouth, and I whimper when he pulls away. *Damn him!* "You haven't come since we opened in January. I want you to experience my newest creation. Plus, you haven't been to one of my restaurants in a long-time Kitten."

The mild accusation snaps me out of my wanton bliss. "Well, someone was avoiding me all year. How was I going to come with no invite?" He opens his mouth to protest, but I hold up my hand, signaling him to save it. "Riddick, I'd love to go, but Raleigh is a good 40 minutes away. Do you really want to drive all that way for dinner? Plus, you live out there. I will have to drive back here to Abbott Ridge in the dark. You know how I feel about driving in the dark."

He grabs me and brushes his firm hands up and down my

arms. I look around, knowing my sisters are going to pour out of our meeting any minute now. This is not a good look. But Riddick doesn't seem to be in any hurry. "I know, and I never expected you to drive back tonight. You will stay with me, like you usually do when you come up."

I laugh and push back against his chest to escape those hands. "Oh no! We are not having a sleepover after the things that went down yesterday and the day before. We need to talk about all this calmly with no sexual interruptions!"

He cocks his head to the side. "Which thing? When you accused me of only wanting to fuck you? Or when you sucked my dick until I came down your throat in your old dorm room? Or maybe you're speaking about how the act of making me explode caused you to combust in your own pants?"

My breathing kicks up and my protest ends in a trapped whimper. His words touch me where I need them most...in my core.

He stalks closer and turns me around before backing me against his Tesla. Now he's a predator admiring his prey. I try to look away, but I can't. He's too damn pretty. The intensity in his eyes is too much and I feel naked. I'm exposed and seen for what I really am; a woman who wants to jump his bones. After an eternity, he finally speaks.

"I may have started us down this road of desire, but giving pleasure is a two-way street." He steps closer until his warm breath caresses my ear. "And that's what you experience with me Brandi, pleasure. Isn't it? Didn't you enjoy coming undone and creaming all over my hand on Friday night? Watching me lick every drop of your sweet juices off my fingers and palm; proving to you just how sweet you really are?"

Jesus, that mouth. It's filthy. I'm wet as a river right now.

He steps back and watches my reaction to his words. No doubt my pupils are dilated. He knows I want him and that his words turned me on. He reaches out and gathers my hair in a ponytail before laying it over my right shoulder. The move is so intimate that I go a little weak in the knees. He's treating me like the fine 150-year-old China my grandmother babies and puts on display.

"Don't worry Brandi, you're still in control. I'm not mad at you for your outburst yesterday and nothing will happen tonight that you don't ask for. I only want to show you my pride and joy and share a good meal with the woman that means the most to me in my life. My best friend, and hopefully one day lover. I'm over lying to myself and you about that. Yes, I want to make love to you. I want to fill-you up to the point of no return. You should be so far gone that you won't know where you start and where I begin. I want you wet and willing beneath me until you're so blissed out that you truly believe the world is your oyster. But none of that will happen if you don't want it to, and I'll still love you."

"I was childish to stay away from you this year. I should have just been honest with you. But I want you to know that the love I have for you now, as my friend, will never change. If you don't feel the same way about me; I will continue to be your friend. I can deal; don't think for a second that I would ever abandon you. You're too important to me for that. Do you understand?"

His last words come out like a small growl, and I know he means it. I'm in control and only what I want to happen will happen. The problem is, I want him just as much as he wants me. But my wish is forever, and I don't know how long this promise will be. It's never been long with anyone else. Am I so different? I always thought what made me different was the fact that we were never sexually connected. Now, I'm not so sure. I take a deep breath and grab his hand.

"Alright, let's go eat. But I'm making no promises about my sleeping arrangements tonight. Deal?"

He smiles and places a kiss on the inside of my wrist. "Deal. Let's go, you can follow behind me. Just keep up, no slow driving. They've increased the speed limit on Interstate 40 and now is the time for a little speed, Kitten."

He winks and walks over to the driver's side of his car while motioning for me to get going.

He's so bossy, but for the first time, I want to be bossed.

Riddick is taking over my heart and I just hope he knows what he's doing.

Because I don't.

Chapter 17

Yes, Impress Me

Riddick

SHE'S DOWN FOR WHATEVER.

To say my latest restaurant, *Busu*, impressed Brandi Armstrong, would be an understatement.

I knew she would love it, but her response went beyond my high expectations. The smell of South African spices and the sounds of my homeland enraptured her. Her smile pleased me down to my toes. As she walked in, her hips swayed to the sounds of Sauti Sol's *Feel My Love*, and I was hypnotized with the movements.

Each of my restaurants has a theme, but the one in Raleigh is the closest to my heart. It's an homage to the very heartbeat of South Africa and Cape Town. My hometown is a dazzling point on the map that, sadly, most Americas never see. So, I brought Cape Town to North Carolina. The moment you step inside, the environment transports you across the world.

We used textiles the color of the blue and green beaches Cape Town is known for. The blue silk covering the booth seating contrasts beautifully with the golden brass and wood tables, reminding you of the sand and water. My cuisine is as rich and varied as Cape Town's overall culture, which blends cultures from all over Africa, Europe, Asia, and even America.

Cape Town is the best of what the entire world offers in one gorgeous city. That's what I attempted to capture in this restaurant.

"Breathtaking," was her description once we sat down and started sampling a wine list starring wines from Cape Town's infamous winelands. During our visit, Brandi sampled everything on the menu. She dared and downed at least three glasses of what is now her favorite wine, a 2017 Nicolas Van Der Merwe Cabernet. I cut her off after the third glass. I needed Brandi relaxed but alert and in full control of her sensibilities for what I have planned for us tonight.

I took a gamble surprising Brandi outside of her book club meeting tonight. I know her well enough to know that she hates to be surprised and that she's nervous about us. But I wanted an open and vulnerable Brandi tonight, not one so hell bent on control that she shuts me out before I even get out of the gate. I didn't want to go to Antonio's, eat greasy pizza, and listen to her give me some weak apology I don't need.

She's scared because her heart's been broken before, and she thinks I lied by omission about my plans for Edenton Shores. She's also not sure about me because I've been a bit of a Casanova in my past. Shit, that's fair, but I would never be that with her. If she gave me the chance to make her mine, I'd never betray her trust. She's, my world.

I brought her to Busu to make her smile and bring that wall down she erects whenever her pussy gets wet. I also brought her because I want her to see the magic I create in my restaurants. If I'm going to talk her into letting me help Edenton Shores by investing and creating a restaurant there, she must believe it's worth the risk.

Brandi hates asking for help, and us turning into more than friends does not help my case. She will not like the idea of mixing business with pleasure. She feels relationships are too fragile to withstand that kind of pressure. Her last relationship caused her to change her life plans and then crashed and burned. So yeah, this will be an uphill battle. But Brandi and her family need me, and I won't fail.

Tonight, I just want to taste her and show her how good it can be between us. That's why I brought her to my home.

Currently, she's showering in the bathroom suite next to the guest room she always sleeps in when she stays the night here. But I have no plans of letting her hide away in there. Tonight, she will be in my bed and sleeping in my arms.

I'm in the kitchen making her favorite snack, some homemade pralines I made last night in anticipation of this visit and a bottle of a 2009 German Riesling by Dr. Heidemanns; I introduced her to three years ago for her birthday. It's not cheap, about $250 a bottle, so she never buys it for herself, but that's why I'm here. *To spoil her rotten.*

When I hear the bathroom door open, I move the tray of pralines and wine out into the family room on a table in front of the fireplace. I'm proud of my place. Brandi calls it Masculine Coastal Chic; whatever that's supposed to mean. But I live on a lake because I always need water near me. I decorated the inside of my home in dark woods, navy, and sea blues with cream accents. The colors calm me, and my home is my sanctuary.

I do not invite women into my home; I prefer to fuck and entertain at theirs. It's simpler that way. But Brandi is always welcome here. Seeing her walking towards me now in my Abbott Ridge College T-shirt and gym shorts makes her look right at home.

"Thanks for the clothes, Riddick. I wasn't prepared to spend the night away from home." Her husky voice makes my dick twitch. She looks incredible with her hair pulled up in a messy topknot and her mahogany skin free of make-up. She's fresh and fuckable. Part of me feels like I'm committing a mortal sin thinking about Brandi this way, but if I'm wrong, I refuse to be right. Brandi is mine; my job tonight is to convince her it's a good thing to belong to me.

"It's my pleasure to clothe you, Brandi. I enjoy seeing you in my things; it makes you look like mine."

I never knew a woman with her complexion could blush, but damn if her cheeks don't have a pinch of fire at the top. She tilts her head to one side and eyes me carefully. "Is that what you really want? To make me yours?"

I chuckle. "I don't know how many times I must tell you that Kitten until you believe me, but yes; that is what I want. Why don't you come over to the couch and join me for some pralines and wine? I'll tell you all about my plans to make you mine."

Her eyes widen, and she groans as she moves towards me. "Riddick, you're not playing fair. You know how I feel about your pralines." When she sees the wine bottle, she grabs it and squeals in delight as she drops into the plush cream couch. I turn to use a remote to start a fire in the gas fireplace in front of us. "Riddick, you got me the German wine! This is so sweet."

I smile as I join her on the couch with two wine glasses I picked up off the table. I love how she eats with no reservations with me. She forgets all about her stupid calorie count, and focuses on what will make her happy. "Of course, I did. I have a bottle or two you can take home with you, too. Your birthday is in two weeks; so, think of it as an early part of your present." I take the wine bottle from her and pour us each a glass before setting the bottle down on the live oak coffee table.

Her black eyes flash with mischief. "Part of my present? Riddick, this is a $250 bottle of wine. I think this alone is a very generous gift. And don't even get me started on that Louis bag you bought me."

I laugh. "You're going to have to get used to having access to my wealth, Brandi. My restaurants have made me a very wealthy man. That bottle of wine is inconsequential to my bank account. But it's priceless because it puts a smile on your face. Understand?"

Brandi's mouth is slightly agape in surprise. She closes it and takes a swig of the delicious wine. Again, I chuckle, because she's

Louise Lennox

still getting used to this side of me- *the warm demander.* Wait until she finds out what I demand in the bedroom.

Once she gathers her nerves, she clears her throat and sticks her feet underneath her. I'm pleased she's relaxing.

"OK Riddick, just how rich are you? I mean, I always knew you were a man of means. Your parents have money, and your restaurants are wildly popular. Even The Fall Line in town burst at the seams every night."

She rears back slightly when she asks, like she's afraid of the answer. I've spent my entire life wealthy and know that women respond to my wealth in one of two ways. They are impressed by it or scared of it. There's rarely an in between. I did not plan to discuss my net worth with Brandi tonight, but if she really wants to know; I'll tell her.

"Are you sure you want to know?"

She smirks. "It's that bad, huh?"

I grin. "You tell me. I am worth about $250 million in liquid assets. My family trust holds three times that, not to mention stock options and real estate investments. So, I don't know a little over a billion." I shrug and knock back the rest of my wine and pour myself another glass. I hate talking about my money, especially with Brandi. My money is the least of what I can offer her.

"Damn Riddick! I did not know you were that rich! What the hell?"

I shrug. "You never asked?"

She snorts. "It never mattered before."

I pin her with my eyes. "Why does it matter now?" *Come on, say it...*

She clears her throat and leans over to pop a praline in her mouth, essentially ending that line of questioning. I exhale, "I don't know why. I guess never wanted you to feel weird around me because of my wealth. If you ever needed anything, I wouldn't hesitate to give you the world. Since I knew that, I never thought I needed to discuss the details of my bank account. It makes good people like you uncomfortable because you don't give a damn about it."

She laughs and swallows. "No, I don't, but I care about you. Being wealthy is a facet of your personality because you have access to that kind of money. Maybe I feel like I don't know you as well as I thought I did? I don't know, I figured you were worth a couple of million, but Riddick, you're damn near a billionaire!"

Actually, I am one, but who's counting?

I nod and put my glass of wine down. I move closer to her and wipe an errant strand of hair from her top knot behind her ear. "Brandi, I want you to hear my heart when I say this. That money doesn't hold a candle to your smile. When you're in my orbit and happy, I feel like a truly rich man. You're my center; my axis. I can only be as happy as you are. I need you to be loved and full of light. Every day, I call you to make sure your day goes well, because I need to know to continue mine. You are my heartbeat in human form, and I want a real chance to show you how a love like that can enhance your life."

Her voice rasps, "Really? Why me? Why do you care about me Riddick, you could have any woman in the word you want? Hell, I'm not so sure you haven't. No offense…"

I rub my thumb over the pad of her bottom lip and smile. "None taken. Yes, Kitten, I've been around. But none of them can hold a candle to you. As Zora Neale Hurston had Teacake tell Janie in Their Eyes Were Watching God, *you hold the keys to the kingdom.* I was out there trying to satisfy myself with imposters because the real thing told me she didn't want love, passion, and companionship, and I took you at your word. But now I know that was foolish."

"I should have done the opposite, Brandelyn Armstrong. I should have told you every day how much I love you and reminded you that you're mine. I should have told you that whenever you're ready, I'll be right here, ready to rock your world to the beat of my heart. I should have kissed you until you were wet and weak in the knees. I should have claimed you."

Her eyes turn into black dots floating in a sea of white and her breathing picks up. She never leaves my gaze. Her pants increase as I apply more pressure to the caress of her lip, and just when I think she's too shocked to say anything, she surprises the shit out of me. She slips her tongue out and pulls my thumb into her mouth. When she releases it with a pop, she sits up on her knees and whispers three words that change everything.

"Claim me now."

Chapter 18

Yes, Claim Me

Riddick

"I'll claim every inch of you."

My campaign starts with a soft kiss to the top of her head. I'm vibrating with need and anticipation. It's time to touch every inch of the woman I've dreamed about for almost two decades. *With no limits.* Quietly, I hum to calm down. I need to last and to remember each moment of this night.

The soft strands of her hair are like silk against my skin. When I run my hands through the strands of the softest coils on earth; her sweet-smelling shampoo fills my nostrils with delight. Reverently, I plant kisses on her forehead, cheeks and nose; not leaving an inch uncovered.

Mine.

I will taste every inch of her until she's damp and covered with my scent.

My lips reach her right ear and I lick around the outer perimeter before taking a bite of her earlobe. She squeals in painful pleasure, and I chuckle. "Do you like that Kitten?"

Brandi's voice is shaky, but she answers. "Y-yes, but it hurts."

"Mmm Hmm" I hum in response. "Yes, but pain and pleasure will be partners in promising you the most mind-blowing orgasm of your life."

I push back to look at her beautiful face. Her big black pools of lust turn away from me. But she can't hide from me. I witnessed equal parts yearning and panic in her eyes. My kitten fears this moment and the aftermath because she knows there's no turning back for us now. Inch by inch, over the past three days, I stripped her control over this situation. Slowly, I walked her to this moment, and I want her to be very present. Brandi will remember the moment I made her mine. She shouldn't feel uncomfortable in her skin. I want the same badass confidence she employs in the courtroom in my bed. I place my index finger under her chin and tenderly force her to look me in my eyes.

"Do you trust me, Kitten?"

"With my life." The conviction of her answer makes my cock swell. This girl can have me for a dime right now.

"Then let me make you feel good inside and out. I know it's been a while since you've been with a man, but I promise you nothing but bliss and an overflow of passion and pleasure. Let me lead."

She searches my eyes for anything other than the truth but doesn't find any deception. Finally, she nods, and I move off the couch to stand in front of her and offer my hand. "Come, I want you to stand in front of the fire."

Brandi obeys right away, and I'm pleased. When she gets to the fireplace, the back glow makes her look like an angel.

"Take off your clothes, Kitten. I want to see all of you."

Her eyes widen, and she hesitates. "Why?" She stammers.

I chuckle, "Because I want to admire what's mine. Don't be shy, your body is a work of art. Brandi, I've fantasized about running my hands over every edge of your sexy frame, so please get out of your head. There's nothing you can do to displease me at this moment. Let me see you."

She swallows and nods before slipping my shirt over her head. She wasn't wearing a bra, and the heaviness of her breasts catch me off guard. *They're beautiful.* She's aroused and her hard nipples stand like dark blueberries against the soft warm brown of her flesh. I gasp when she grabs them and twists. She looks me straight in my eyes, bites her lips and releases a moan.

Well, that was unexpected. I'm game.

I stand and walk towards her, forcing my feet not to rush. When we were backstage at the gymnasium, I overwhelmed her. Now I want to seduce her; show her how exacting I can be. I slip my shirt over my head and toss it to the side. When I'm finally face to face with her, I can see the desire in her eyes. She wants this just as bad as I do, and nothing is more of a turn on than that.

I rub my hands together and drink her in. "Brandi, I will ask your consent at every step of tonight's journey. You must tell me exactly what you want and what you don't want. I need your explicit trust and communication for this to work. Do you understand?"

Eagerly she nods and I waste no more time. "My tongue is going to explore all of you while you're standing here looking sexy as fuck in this firelight. If you need something to hold on to, use me. Ready?"

She shoots me a needy look bordering on frustration. "Riddick, just taste me already. I'm dying over here waiting."

I chuckle and grab the firm mounds of her juicy ass to drag her body against mine. My hands move her up and down my hard length while I take her mouth in a firm kiss. She should feel what she does to me. My kiss demands she lets go of the past hurts and throw herself fully into what the present and future offer-me. When I let go to come up for air, her breathing is a heavy pant, and she has a wild look in her eyes.

I don't waste another minute and wipe my tongue out over her left nipple while my hand massages her right breast. My tongue laves gently over the hard flesh. I bite down and relish in her squeal. My tongue soothes the area of pain and I take her entire breast in my mouth to suck while I pinch her right nipple. The pressure makes her squirm and her hands land on my shoulders for support.

I move to her next breast and repeat the production of pleasure but this time when I bite down, her scream is more of a pleasurable squeal; she was ready for my touch.

She's responding beautifully.

Back and forth I go, greedily consuming her breasts like the gourmet meals I prepare. Her skin tastes like heaven, and I never want to come down.

I release her breast with a pop of my lips and lick down the center of her chest until I reach her soft stomach. I love that she's not hard and angular, but her stomach has the forgiving flesh of a woman. There's no need for her to do 100 sit-ups a day or lift weights in a gym. Brandi's body is a work of art without her even trying.

Dropping to my knees, my tongue circles her belly button, dipping in, out, and around. I look up at her when I make it to the apex of her thighs. My hands lightly spread her legs. I lean forward and place my nose at her wet center. Closing my eyes, I inhale her scent to smell her essence.

A groan escapes from the back of my throat; her scent causes my cock to leak into my sweatpants. *She's fucking incredible.* On my knees I look up at her and prepare to worship.

I drag my finger over her closed folds. "Are you going to let me eat this little pussy, Kitten?"

There is no air... so there are no words. She says nothing. Instead, her breathing speeds up. I tease her pussy lips with a light graze from my fingers. "Hmm? Can I part your brown lips and look at your pretty center? Can I touch you there?"

She can't answer, and I eye the wetness dripping down her thighs. There's a soft tremble in her thighs and I realize what's happening when a moan escapes.

She's ready to come.

I slap her pussy three times in rapid succession to slow her down and drive her fucking crazy.

"Riddick!" She half moans and half curses.

"Answer me, Brandi. What do you want me to do to this wet pussy? It's wet and leaking for me, isn't it? I lick up the side of her thigh and taste her cream. "This is for me, isn't it? Your sweet cream belongs to me. Tell me sweet Brandi. Are you dripping for me?"

Her breathing slows down, and she shakes before she speaks. "Yes... Lick me Riddick. Please."

Yes. Love. I. Will.

Her voice is soft but strong. I stand and lift her up, placing her legs around my waist. I carry us to the nearest wall and press her body against it before dropping to my knees again. My hand holds her in place against the wall by her ass cheeks and my forearms lift and stretch her wide.

"Relax." I command, and she obeys while my hands still massage her ass. She opens wider for me, pushing her thighs as far as they can go, while holding on to my shoulders. My lips stroke up and down her dripping brown folds and separate them to expose the pink essence underneath. Slowly, my tongue licks her from the bottom of her pussy to the top, stopping at her hard clit and biting down. Her hands immediately go into my hair, and she shutters.

"Yes Kitten, come apart for me." I lick again, repeating the gesture while my hands explore her ass. My finger coasts around her dark hole and I know she's not ready for that. However, I press there, letting her know that someday I'm going to show her how pleasurable that place can be.

"Hold on to me baby," I whisper before I French kiss her portal of pleasure and push my tongue inside her. The sounds Brandi make are unlike anything I've ever heard. She's letting go, she's allowing her body to give over to my attention, and I'm overjoyed. I lick. I suck. I bite. I tease. She is a bowl of my homemade praline ice cream dripping with caramel syrup. When she rocks, I know she's about to come and can't hold back any longer. *Good, I'm ready to taste her.*

I land a bite to the inside of her thigh and kiss the mark to bring her attention back to me.

"You need to come, Kitten?"

She catches my eyes as I look up to plead. "Yes, Riddick please. Make me come"

With. Pleasure.

I thrust one finger inside her pussy and continue to lick her every inch of her core. When I pump in and out of her wet center, the wet sounds take over the room. She's dripping and I add another finger, satisfied when I hear the delicious groan she gives. *She's close.* Her thighs squeeze against my head, but it doesn't stop me-instead it centers me. I move my focus totally to her hard, throbbing clit and I slurp hard before adding a third finger to fuck her with. My index finger curls up against that sweet, rough spot I introduced her to Friday night.

The high-pitched scream and the cream gushing from her, tells me I've hit the jackpot. I drink every drop, quenching my thirst for a woman that's brought joy to my life for almost twenty years. There will never be another one like her. I don't waste one drop of her honeyed essence and pump her through one orgasm after the other. She's riding a wave of pleasure that could last forever, but I need to come up for air.

Finally, I smack her ass to alert her it's time to come down from her high. This is only the start of our night and there's so much more to do. When she finishes with a shudder, I stand up and carry her to the couch where we started.

I lay her back on leather throw pillows and she looks sated. Her eyes are closed while she catches her breath. I use the time to remove her shorts and the rest of my clothes. Her eyes pop open once I'm naked and she drinks me in. Her eyes dilate. She likes what she sees. Her hand reaches out and skates over my hard stomach.

"Riddick, you're beautiful," she murmurs.

My heart drops into my chest. "No Kitten, you are. You're exquisite. My diamond."

She looks up at me, and a tear falls out of her eye. She swallows and continues to rub her hand up and down my stomach.

"Can I taste you?"

I stumble back. Of all the things that she could say right now, that is not what I expected to hear. I want nothing more than to feel her mouth on my cock again. I tilt my head to the side and study her.

"You want my cock in your mouth?"

Brandi nods eagerly and sits up. "Yes, more than anything. Please let me taste you."

Well, hot damn…

Chapter 19

Yes, Taste Me
Brandi

PLEASE, let me taste you...

Who am I right now? Shit, who was I yesterday in that dorm room? I've never been so brazen in my life. Between the blinding orgasm Riddick just gave me and my comfort level with him, I feel powerful enough to ask for anything I want. I can even beg if that's my prerogative. Right now, I want that lead pipe he calls a cock filling my mouth to its limit.

Then he can fuck me senseless. It's been almost twenty years, and it feels appropriate that I break my fast with him. And I do mean break. I want him to ruin me for every other man on earth. I want to be nothing but a pile of pleasured bones when we're done. Riddick's been by my side throughout the drought. He kept me satisfied with his love and care alone. Even when I drove him crazy, he was a constant source of joy in my life. My family's farm was in trouble, and he's found a way to hold us down. He did that for me, and I'll love him for life because of it.

He breaks me down to my best form.

I'm becoming his in every way possible. I'm not scared. He's proven to me I'm his priority, so I won't hold back another minute.

I scoot to sit on the edge of the couch and spread my legs. He watches me before stepping between my thighs with a ready cock pointing straight at me. The large bull makes me wet as a river again. Riddick's nostrils flare, and his fists clench his sides. His jaw is clenched tight, and the man looks ready to explode. I dart my tongue out to lick the bead of pre-cum from his leaking tip and his breath releases a roar.

Raging Bull. Meet the red flag.

He grabs my jaw and firmly pushes it down. "Stick your tongue out again, but this time, hold your position. I'm going to fuck your mouth, Kitten. Are you ready?"

I look up at his naked form and moan. He's built like an inked Greek God, and I want to taste every line and ridge of him. I wish I could take my time, but I'm too horny right now. I want to make it good for him. If it's good for him, it will be explosive for me.

His thick column pushes heavy against my tongue as he slides in. He's slow at first, testing my limits. He pushes his cock to the back of my throat, and I open up to swallow him down. I cough, but he uses his other hand to stroke my neck, not giving me an inch of reprieve. I swallow around him again and he slides further and further until I gag and sputter. Tears roll down my eyes and I'm sure my face is a sloppy mess. But who cares?

He pulls his cock out of my mouth like it's on fire and hisses before pushing in against my tongue again.

"That's it, Kitten. Take all of me. I want you to swallow every inch of this dick down. It's all for you..."

His last word trails off as he groans when my nose hits his stomach. His skin smells divine. *Money. Musk. Man.*

"Fuck Brandi, I can't hold back. Your mouth drives me crazy. Keep your mouth open. Don't close it for shit!"

Both his hands cradle my head and he pistons his hips. He's giving me a preview of how he will take my pussy and I'm wet as a stream in Spring. I disobey him and close my mouth over his length; sucking hard as his dick pushes in. His knees slightly buckle. I want his cum, and I plan to suck him until he gives it to me. The quicker he comes down my throat; the quicker the main event begins.

But Riddick has other plans.

He pulls out my mouth with a pop and lifts me up by my under arms. He cradles me to his chest, and I feel the strong beat of his heart. "Where are we going?"

"To my bed. I need to be inside of you now. The next time I come, I will be between your naked thighs and releasing within the walls of that sweet pussy of yours."

Oh...

"Wait Riddick, I'm not on the pill. I never needed it before. Do you have condoms?"

He pauses in the hallway and looks at me. I turn shy and turn into his chest to hide. "Look at me Brandi." I pull my face away from his chest. "I'm clean, and I'm a grown ass man with more money than a false god. I really don't care if I give you babies. You are it for me. Once I make you mine, there will be no other women. There haven't been for almost a year. I want you swollen and heavy with my child. Are you ready for that?"

I don't have to think for long. *Hell Yes, I want that.* I nod and whisper, "Yes."

He places a kiss on my forehead and squeezes me tight before moving towards our destination.

Once we get to his bedroom; I look around in awe. I've never really been inside his sanctum. This moment is a milestone. He never invited me in here, even when I stayed over. I was always curious, but we both knew coming into his bedroom would cross a line of intimacy we weren't ready to consummate.

Tonight, his blue and gold-colored haven feels like home. Like the family room, there is a fireplace burning brightly to illuminate the space. He drops me in the center of the bed on a duvet soft as Cotton Candy. I sit up on my elbows to study the tribal tattoos swirling around his chest and arms. His body is truly a badass work of art.

But it's the way he's looking at me that takes my breath away.

He stares at me like I'm the only thing in his universe worth viewing. The awe in his eyes and the hitch in his breath make love to me before he even touches me.

"Open your legs, beautiful. Let me see what's mine."

Moments ago, his face was planted in my pussy. However, this feels different. It's something about lying here open for him that makes me feel truly exposed. I hesitate and he grabs my ankle to scoot me down closer to him.

"Come now, Kitten, show me that pretty pussy; she's purred beautifully for me already. Now I want to reward her and fill her up."

I weep with need and spread wide for him.

He draws a finger down the center of my sex. "That's it, love, hold your thighs open for me. You need to be nice and open because I can't go slow Brandi. I've wanted you too long. But I promise you two things. You will come... hard. And we'll go slow next time."

"I don't need slow Riddick. I need whatever you have. Give it to me."

"Fuck," he groans. His mouth dives into my center and he licks my pussy, turning it back into a stream. When the passionate waters run, he rubs his cock against my folds a few times to gather my juices and lube his cock. He pushes me back onto the bed and removes my arms from my thighs to place them around his neck. Before I register much else, he pushes his thick shaft into me with one powerful thrust and I'm finally full.

God, I'm so full.

He drags his body up and down over mine as he fills me to the brim before he lets go; repeatedly. The friction against my clit makes me see stars. His kisses drop wherever he finds a spot of open skin and the stimulation overworks my body. I shoot off like a rocket, screaming my release.

"Riddick...Oh...God...Riddick..."

"That's it, love, keep coming for me." He drops a bite on my shoulder and pumps faster, causing another wave of pleasure to take over my senses.

"I love you, Brandi. Do you hear me? I. love. You." His balls smack against my ass with every word. "Come again for me Kitten... Come hard on this dick."

He lifts my legs and gathers them over one side of his shoulder to fuck me with no hindrances. "Whose pussy is this, Kitten?"

The pleasure is too intense. Words take much thought. There are only moans, grunts, and tears. I weep with pleasure and breathe him in for oxygen. When he takes my body over the edge yet again; I breathe him in and become high.

He reaches down and kisses me with a punishing force that matches the relentless pounding he's delivering to my pussy until I scream into his mouth. He lets go of my lips and I lose my damn mind to the pleasure as his dick pushes faster and harder into me.

"Tell me Brandi. Who do you belong to? Whose pussy is this?"

"Yours," I sob and scream. "It's yours Riddick."

"Good girl," He grunts and leans down to slap my ass and bites my left cheek. When he stands again, he pushes hard into me one last time and stills. He shakes and when he releases his seed into me; I know it's a sign of forever. I hope his seed plants, because there will be no one else.

This is the man who unwound me from my pain. The man who saw me and loved me without demands.

Riddick is the man who will never let me hunger or thirst again.

He is love.

Chapter 20

Yes, Marry Me

Riddick

SIX MONTHS LATER...

"THEY'RE HERE KITTEN. Are you ready?"

Taking in a deep breath, I shake off my jitters. I left my home in Abbott Ridge four months ago to move in with Riddick in Raleigh. Since I left, I haven't seen anyone in my family. That's not by design; I've just been crazy busy with my new life. I go into my Advocacy Center for work when I need to, but I do most of my work on the road with clients all over the state. When I'm not working; I'm here in Raleigh, making Riddick's house a true home for us.

Tonight, I face Mae for the first time since we had that awful fight at Edenton Shores six months ago. I invited her along with the rest of the family to dinner to make amends.

Once I understood what Riddick and my grandfather planned to do about Edenton Shores, I still wasn't completely on board, but I understood the need. It took me a while to realize that we weren't losing anything. Just because we couldn't afford to function as a working farm anymore didn't mean my family's legacy was lost. It's OK to expand and try new things. Like my grandfather says, if the family is together and taken care of; what we do with the land is inconsequential.

Mae and Darius are extremely hands on with helping Riddick design the menu, plot the winery and hire a staff. The contractors started building the main restaurant structure three months ago, and we should be ready to open by summer. According to Riddick, Mae found her niche in hospitality and management.

Smiling, I reach up on my toes and kiss Riddick's cheek. "I'm more than ready."

With his arm wrapped around my waist, we open the heavy carved-wood door and let my family in. No one has been here before, so their eyes open in wonder as they step into the open and airy foyer. The floors are white marble, and the ceiling is arched and paneled in a deep cognac colored wood. The walls are white and antique gold frames holding black and white photos of them, Riddick's parents, local Black farms, and his family's game reserve line the entryway. I hug my niece and grandfather while Riddick daps up Darius and hugs Mae.

I miss having Ciara here to make everything less awkward with her commanding personality. But she's off running around Africa with Seth Canton. Apparently, he went to college with some Chief in Ghana named Adom Annan. This chief invited him out to spend time with him and his wife, Maya. He wants Seth to open a bar in Accra. Seth asked Ciara to go with him, and I had a fit. I still don't think she knows him well enough to go galli-vanting around the globe. Six months is not a long time. Of course, she disagreed, blew me a kiss, and took off on a private jet across the world. That chick gets on my nerves! But I'm happy for her.

Once everyone's awe of the foyer wears off; my grandfather breaks the ice.

"Boy! I knew you were rich! But what kind of place is this? This is fancier than that place Brandi had in town!"

Riddick laughs. "Welcome to our home, Ellis. And trust me, it looks way better now that Brandi lives here and put her touch on it. It was just a house before, and now it's a home."

My grandfather smiles and slaps Riddick's shoulder and a rare dimple pops out on the left side of my grandfather's cheek. "Yeah, well, that's what a good woman does. She makes wherever you are fell like home. Now, I'm hungry. I hope you all got some food ready in here."

Everyone laughs and makes their way down the hallway to the family room. I reach out and place my hand on Mae's elbow. She whips around with a look of confusion on her face, and I smile.

"Sorry, Mae. I didn't mean to startle you. Can we stay here and talk a moment?"

Riddick looks over his shoulder as he continues to escort everyone else out to get settled and winks at me. *He's pleased.*

Mae nods, but sighs. "Look Brandi, I don't want to fight. I know we may never be as close as we once were, but I think we should at least be civil to one another. I felt guilty about what happened between Byron and me for a long time. But I can't hold on to that anymore. I apologized. I was young and restless. I missed my parents, and I know that's no excuse because you missed yours, too. He just made me believe he could fill that void, if that makes any sense. But it was almost twenty years ago, and I've got to move on. If that means we will never be cool; then so be it."

I shake my head and pull Mae into a strong hug. She whelps in surprise and stays stiff as a board for a few moments. Then she finally relents and hugs me back when she hears me whisper, "I'm so sorry."

We pull back and unshed tears brim both our eyes. "Mae, I'm so sorry. Unforgiveness lingered in my heart for so long that it spilled onto my feelings for you. I never hated you. I just thought if I forgave you, it would be like admitting what he did to me was no big deal. To be honest, I should have forgiven him a long time ago too, because I let him still matter in my life by holding on to that hatred. If I had truly let go, maybe I would have found my happiness with Riddick a lot sooner."

I sniffle when Mae reaches out to squeeze my hand. "Mae, I'm so sorry about the way I acted. I'm sorry for accusing you of robbing the family and the farm. I love you and I want us to rebuild our relationship and forget that Byron ever existed."

Mae nods. "I'd like that, Brandi. You do not know how long I've wanted this. I was hoping you would come to some of the design meetings with Riddick, so you could see what we're turning Edenton Shores into. I feel like I've found what I'm supposed to do with the rest of my life."

I squeeze her into a side hug and laugh. "Riddick tells me every week! He's so proud of you, Mae. Shit, I'm proud of you. You should go back to school for hospitality and management! It would be great. You know Abbott Ridge College has an amazing program."

She chuckles. "Girl, I'm too old for that! What am I going to do? Walk to class right alongside Toya every day?"

I turn her around and place my hands on her shoulders. "Yes, Mae. That's exactly what you're going to do. You're not old, you're thirty-seven. Do it!"

She pauses for a moment. Her mouth quirks up into a smile. "You know what? I just might!"

I hug her again until I hear Riddick calling us into the family room. "Girls, come in here. Y'all have got to see this."

Mae and I look at each other and shrug. I take her hand and walk her into the family room, where our 85-inch OLED TV is hanging above the fireplace. It's loud and showing a crystal-clear picture of Byron Logan being escorted, hand cuffed alongside his father.

"What happened?" I gasp.

My grandfather speaks. "Seems that the Logans have been laundering drug money for different gangs through that big tobacco farm of theirs. Byron Sr. and Jr. had their greedy little hands all over it. They would buy properties from struggling farmers; by paying off local banks and speed up the foreclosure process to back them into a corner. They bought the farms for ten cents on the dollar. Then they would use the farms as fronts for the drug money that needed to be cleaned."

"Well, according to the news report, they burned the wrong family. It took the farmer five years, but he finally convinced investigators to go look at his old farm and see that won't nothing growing out there. The Logan's claimed it was still a tobacco farm, but they cooked those books like the steak we about to eat! Looks like the only legitimate business Logan Agricultural Holdings ever did was with you Riddick and a few of those commercial properties he built."

Riddick exhales. "That's because I used to watch him like a hawk to make sure everything was legit. I should have cut ties with that fool a long time ago."

I place a hand over my mouth and shake my head in horror. Once I get over the initial shock of it all, I turn to Riddick. "All those people lost their farms for nothing. He wasn't even doing anything with the land. I couldn't save everyone from Byron. I could only take so many cases. But now I'm determined to help those families get back what they lost. There's got to be a way!"

Riddick kisses me. "Kitten, if there is one. I know you will find it. And if there isn't one. I know you will make it." I reach up and pull him back down into a passionate kiss, releasing a small moan before I let go. *Damn, he's hot.*

"Well, that's enough of this. My grandfather shouts, as he turns the TV off. "That scum will get what he deserves. Can we eat now? I'm too old to wait for my meals."

Riddick laughs. "Of course, but can I say one thing before we head to the dining room?"

My grandfather sighs. "Lord. Please hurry before I die."

I chuckle. "What is it, babe? You know Ellis Armstrong doesn't play with his stomach."

Riddick pulls a small blue box from his pocket and beams at me with a true twinkle in his eye. Before I can ask him what he's up to. The man drops to one knee and opens the box to reveal a pear-shaped diamond solitaire surrounded by green emeralds on a platinum band.

"Kitten. You've made my life complete. I want you to be spiritually, sexually, and legally all mine for the rest of my life. Will you marry me?"

I pause in shock. Can my life really be the greatest romance novel written? Do I really get the hot guy, hot sex, and a Happily Ever After? The answer is yes... yes; I freaking do!

"Yes," I shout. "Yes, forever and always. Yes!"

He stands and places the ring on my finger. "Kiss me, Kitten."

Without question, I obey.

THE END.

Two Years Later

Brandi

"Are you nervous Kitten?"

I look in the bathroom vanity mirror and smile at my delicious husband. We've been married for 365 glorious days and I'm so happy that I could burst. He's standing behind me, fresh out of the shower, and his naked chest makes my mouth water.

"No love, what makes you ask?"

Riddick laughs. "I know little about make-up, but I'm pretty sure you don't want the left one painted silver, and the right one to sport gold shadow."

I look up in the mirror and mutter a curse. Then I shake my head at my beautiful mate and laugh. "Ok, I may be a little nervous. It's not every day a girl opens a restaurant and winery with her family. I know this is number eight for you, including The Fall Line Bar, but I'm geeked. This restaurant is the best anniversary gift ever."

A little over two years ago, Riddick saved our family farm, Edenton Shores, by paying off mortgages on the land and helping us turn it into a farm-to-table culinary destination and winery. The land is still owned by my grandfather Ellis and our family, but Riddick splits the profits from the restaurant with us.

First, I was against turning our farm into a restaurant. There

Louise Lennox

are too few working Black owned farms in America. But once I realized what mattered was keeping ownership and serving our community any way we can; I opened to the idea. Riddick has six successful restaurants and one bar; he knows how to make this a success. The buzz has been bananas. The publicity is great, but it also makes me nervous.

Riddick places a soft kiss on each of my shoulders before biting my ear lobe. "Everything is going to be fine, Brandi. We're ready for this. *Ma Kate's Food and Winery* will be a hit and make the memory of your grandmother proud. Mae and her team worked very hard to make it an incredible dining experience as soon as you step on the property. Wait until you see it."

I huff. "I wouldn't have to wait, if y'all hadn't banned me from stepping foot on the property until tonight."

I'm still peeved about that.

Riddick's chuckle loosens the tension in my stomach. My best friend turned lover can turn my mood around with just one sound.

Sexual sorcery at its finest.

"Kitten, if you weren't such a bossy brat, we would have gladly welcomed you at the site. Admit it, love, it's hard for you to function in a space you're not in control of. You have what your grandfather calls, "a take over spirit" It's OK, it's part of the reason I love you."

I stomp my foot. "I was not a brat!" My protest doesn't hold much weight since I barely believe it myself. I was a lot to deal with at the start of development. Everything had to be beyond perfect if we were giving up the ideal of having a working farm. I also felt we owed something spectacular to the community of Abbott Ridge.

Riddick turns me around and unties the knot of my robe. The look he gives me is liquid sex. "Yes, you were. I had to get you out of there before you and Mae had another fight that lasted almost two decades. Now, let's stop talking about all of that and get you naked. I want to fuck my wife."

I scoff. "You don't want to make love to your wife?"

Riddick shakes his head and slips my stain robe off my shoulders. "No, she knows I love her. This isn't about the copious amounts of love I heap on her daily. This is about calming her nerves, and only a good fuck will do that."

Well Damn.

I nuzzle him away. "Won't we be late? The opening starts in an hour."

Riddick winks and twirls me around. "Kitten, trust me, with the way your body looks in this red thong, it won't take me long at all to tap this beautiful ass of yours. Now be a good girl and place your hands on the counter and put that ass up in the air for me."

He slaps both my ass cheeks, eliciting a moan before I obey.

His towel drops behind me, and the thud makes me salivate like one of Pavlov's damn dogs. He pulls my thong down to my thighs, to hold them close together and in place. When his two fingers drag through my drenched pussy, my knees buckle. Fuck, I already want to come.

Riddick puts a tight grip on my hip and leans over to talk sweet shit in my ear. "You like to be in charge until I bend your sweet ass over and fill you full of my cock. But right now, I'm taking away all your worries baby…"

With one powerful stroke, he pushes into my wet center balls deep and I see stars. It knocks the wind out of me in the best way and I lay my cheek in the cool marble of the sink.

Riddick pulls all the way out, smacks my ass, before pushing to the hilt inside me once again. His slow torture only lasts a few more strokes before he speeds up and fucks me hard. With every stroke, a smack stings my ass and the mix of plain and pleasure rocket me to the moon. The grunts coming from my throat are unrecognizable. The hurt feels too good to think.

"That's right Kitten. Purr for me. I want you to come hard on my dick. I want a waterfall of your creamy essence to make a

Louise Lennox

mess of my cock." The slaps increase with his pace. "Come now Brandi, come hard Kitten."

And I do. All the worry and doubt about the evening washes away with one orgasm after the other. I don't know how long I'm bent over or how many orgasms I ended up having, but when I come too, I'm wrung out like a well-used wash cloth.

Riddick picks me up and cradles me in his arms, whispering every sweet and filthy thing he can imagine. He walks me to our bed and lays me down, kissing me deeply until I fully come back to reality. "Do you feel better about tonight?"

I moan. "Mmmm Hmmm." I give him a sheepish smile and reach up to stroke his cheek. "You're so good to me," I whisper.

Riddick smiles. "I don't deserve you, but since God saw fit to bless me with you; I will spend the rest of my life putting this calm and happy look on your face."

This man. I sit up on my elbows and realize my thong is still wrapped around my thighs. I laugh and pull them up before hopping off the bed. Riddick frowns.

"Where are you going? We have time for at least five minutes to cuddle."

I shake my head. "We really don't. But it doesn't matter. I want to give you your anniversary gift now."

Riddick sits up and rubs his hands together in anticipation. "I thought we were waiting until tomorrow to exchange gifts at our private dinner?"

I nod. "We are. But I want to give you this one now." I pull out an envelope from the nightstand and hand it to Riddick. Puzzled, he opens it and smiles when he sees the ultrasound picture.

He jumps off the bed and shouts. "Kitten! You're pregnant?! We're having a baby?!"

I nod and he leaps over the ottoman at the foot of our bed to grab me and spin me around. "Baby," he roars, "this is the best day of my life." He puts me down and looks me in the eye.

"I will dedicate the rest of my life to making sure you and our

160

child never want for anything. This is what life is all about. Loving you and our child."

I take his face in both my hands and kiss him senseless. When we come up for air, I smile and slide out from his arms. "Ok, we can celebrate more tonight. Right now, we need to get to our restaurant."

Riddick laughs. "Yes, we should get ready. But tonight, I am making love to my wife; all night long."

Ma Kate's Food and Winery took my breath away before we even stepped inside. We drove up about ten minutes ago and at first glance Edenton Shores still looked like home; but better.

Immediately, I saw the twinkling café lights and lanterns stretched along the acres of land. The music from a live soul band warmed my spirit as I bopped to their cover of Maze's *We are One.* I stood proudly in my silk sundress and four-inch wedges and breathed in the night air while I waited for Riddick to complete a call with a bartender about the drink specials for the night. Even with all the hustle and bustle to make the night happen, my skin shivered with the anticipation of a perfect night.

Now that his call is done, Riddick leads me by the hand down a lighted stone path to the main restaurant. The large three-story structure is constructed of enormous stone walls, cognac colored wood beams, columns, and trim; along with large picture glass windows that run to the peaked roof. *It's stunning.*

When I look to the right, I view the largest wood pergola I've ever seen. It covers tables, a massive bar, and a slick stage. The band is jamming, and everyone is drinking, dancing, and having a great time.

To the left of the main restaurant are my grandfather's open fields. The first few acres are clear, with scattered seating and a few trails to walk. The trails lead to the vineyards and gardens. Between the outdoor areas and the bustle inside I can see from the windows, it seems like the entire town of Abbott Ridge is here to celebrate. This is true a community space and I wouldn't have it any other way.

I drop Riddick's hand and spin around with my hands out at my sides. "This is incredible. It's a living dream. I just wish my grandma was still here to see it. She would be delighted. She always thought her wine belonged in stores, and now it's the star of an entire culinary experience."

Riddick grabs me by my waist and places a kiss on the side of my head. "I'm glad you love it. Wait until you go inside. Mae drew inspiration from your grandmother's sense of style and décor. It truly is Ma Kate's winery. Her spirit is present at every touch of the place."

I squeeze his hand. "I can't wait! Let's Go!"

We walk inside the warm and cozy feeling of the space, and it overtakes me. Mae upholstered the barstools at the bar in the same patterns our grandmother used to create throw pillows and draperies. She had an interest in African Art and textiles. She gave up her graduate studies in African Studies when she met my grandfather at Clark Atlanta University.

After graduation, he convinced her to come back to North Carolina and help him work his family's land. She loved him, so she agreed. I don't think she ever regretted her decision, but she never let her interests die. To see her sweet mix of West African and Gullah patterns on the seats and table coverings makes me smile. Even the wallpaper sports one of her designs.

We take a seat at the bar, and I catch Mae flying by. She looks amazing. The days of her Old McDonald Flannel are gone. Tonight, she's striking in a long, black body-clinging sleeveless dress that sports a deep V down the front. The cut hits right above her navel and gives you the perfect peek of her champagne-colored skin. Her hair hangs in natural kinky waves around her face and down her back, with a red lip finishing the look. *She's a boss.*

"Mae!" I call out. Her face flashes with irritation until she realizes I'm the one who called her. An easy smile breaks across her mouth and she walks back.

"Oh my God! I'm so glad you're here! Do you love it Brandi? Did we do a good job?"

Tears prick my eyes. Mae and I had a rocky past. But in the last two years we've done everything we can to become closer. We have a monthly dinner date along with Ciara that we never miss, and I rarely go over two days without talking to her. "Mae, you killed it! I'm so glad ya'll kicked me out of the planning process."

We both laugh and hug. Mae pulls back and takes both my hands in hers. "Girl, me too. Now you've got to try the Fried Green Tomatoes first! They're Ma Kate's recipe."

I nod and give her another quick hug. "Will do!"

She blows me a kiss and skitters away. I'm sure she's more than a little busy tonight. I feel Riddick's warm arms wrap around me from behind, and he nips at my ear. "Is my Kitten pleased with her anniversary present?"

I tip my head back and wrap my hand around the back of his head, pulling him down for a kiss. He meets my lips head-on, and we share a moment of passion in the middle of our family's restaurant.

"Riddick, I'm more than pleased. I'm loved. And it's all because of you."

The Jane Thing

A Best Friend's Sibling Romance

Continue your escape with the next book from the MEET CUTE BOOK CLUB.

The Jane Thing by Tracy Broemmer
Meet Cute Book Club, *Book #2*
Releasing on June 30, 2022

When my best friend asks me to put her brother up at my place for a while, I'm totally on board. After all, I practically grew up in Chloe and Gideon's house, so I used to kind of know him. Those childhood memories don't compare to the real Gideon Reece when he shows up ready to be my temporary roommate. He's grown into a smoking hot guy complete with tattoos, rakish-looking hair, and a face that looks like art. Too bad he's a pompous jerk.

My sister's best friend is going to drive me crazy before my stay here is over. She's prettier than I remember, but she's all sunshine and chatter, like she thinks we're going to be besties while I'm here. Spoiler alert: we're not. I'm here to secure a job and find a place to live, and in the meantime, I have no interest in palling around with Skye Stafford.

Then why did I kiss her? Probably the same reason I can't get her off my mind. She's completely different from any woman I've ever known, and to my regret, I can't get enough of her. I have to keep my hands to myself, because I'd never forgive myself if I came between Chloe and Skye.

Meet Cute Book Club Series

Escape with the Meet Cute Book Club where meet-cutes don't only happen between the pages of romance novels and members find their own happily ever afters. Eight single women bound by their love of books take a monthly break from real life to lose themselves in the chapters of romantic fiction.

These eight standalone romances are packed with meet-cutes, heat, and of course a happily ever after!

The Wine Down by Louise Lennox
A Friends to Lovers Romance

The Jane Thing by Tracy Broemmer
A Best Friend's Sibling Romance

The Forever Game by A.M. Williams
A Sports Romance

The Right Guy by Mel Walker
A Fake Relationship Romance

The Hidden Love by RJ Gray
A Second Chance Romance

The Mix Up by Rebecca Wilder
A Grumpy Sunshine Romance

The Hometown Dilemma by Julie Archer
A Return to Hometown Romance

The Book Boyfriend by Kate Stacy
A Wrong Side of the Tracks Romance

Also By Louise Lennox

The Kiawah Kisses Series

Merry Kiss Me, Rhue &Symone

Kiss of Life, Cameron &Tara

Kiss of Fate, Ray & Nicole

Kiss of Karma, Richard & Keisha

The Passionate Professors Duet

Love & Lyrics-Book 1- Luke & Raina

Love & Lipstick,Book 2- Peter & Mia

The Sexy Sovereign Series: Ashanti Royalty

Craving a King,Book 1- Kofi & Ella

Choosing the Chief,Book 2- Adom & Maya

Possessing the Prince,Book 3- Senya and Abena

Standalone Romance(s)

Savannah's Salvation-Michael & Savannah

Stay Connected

Subscribe to my Newsletter!

My newsletter has new release updates, recipes, book reviews, free books by other authors, and much more!

Follow Me!

I am in LOVE with Instagram. Keep up with all that goes on in my world; including exclusive content from upcoming books @author-louiselennox!

I am very active on GoodReads-Follow me for signed copy give-aways, book recommendations, and reviews!

We have a fun and active #HappyBlackRomance Readers Group on Facebook! Join Us!We discuss all things Happy, Black, and Romantic!

Finally, I am building my BookBub Platform. If you use the site follow me there too for book recommendations!

Acknowledgments

My Husband and Children: K...You already know what it is. Thank You for reading every chapter I write and providing feedback every night...until Midnight. You dear are the real M.V.P.

To my 2 babies: thank you for being you. You make me want to be better and do bigger!

My Parents: Thank you for convincing me I can do all things through CHRIST that strengthens me. Because of your teachings; I'm not afraid of a thing!

My Spelman Sisters: Our Spelman Moms group provides so much support. We are all so successful and busy; yet in our group, we can cry, yell, and laugh. Thank You for volunteering to be BETA readers. Thank You for being my ARC team. Thank You for starting me out on social media. Thank You for believing in me. We will forever remain #undaunted.

Thanks to every professional editor , cover designer, and formatter. We did it! AGAIN!

God Bless,

Louise

About the Author

Contemporary romance author Louise Lennox is a hopeful romantic writing steamy romances full of heart and healing.
A Spelman College and Georgetown University graduate, she launched #HappyBlackRomance; a community of readers and writers committed to the creation and sharing of positive romance stories featuring Black heroines.
Louise Lennox plots highlight the joys of Black relationships across the diaspora; pushing readers from all cultural backgrounds to admire them for their strength and downright sexiness. In her novels sparks always fly; the sex amazes; and the characters always leave the world better than they found it through their love.
When she's not writing, Louise is enjoying her work as a school leader, wife, and mother of the two cutest dragons to ever walk the earth!
To learn more about #HappyBlackRomance and to score a free book or two, check out her website www.lovelouiselennox.com